JUNE FOSTER

Flawless

Woodlyn, Book 1

By June Foster

Copyright © 2018 by June Foster

Forget Me Not Romances, a division of Winged Publications.

All rights reserved as permitted under the U.S. Copyright Act of 1976. No part of the publication may be reproduced, distributed or transmitted in any form or by any means, or stored in a database or retrieval system, without prior permission of the publisher.

This book is a work of fiction. Names, characters, places, and incidents are the product of the author's imagination and are used fictitiously. Any resemblance to actual events, locales, or persons, living or dead, is coincidental.

All rights reserved.

ISBN-13: 979-8-8690-2092-5

Chapter One

The overweight guy leaning against the mirror in the corner of the elevator caught Holly Harrison's attention, not because of his girth, but because of the kindness on his chubby face. Embarrassed she'd stared too long, she turned toward the closing doors and pushed *five*. The motor whirred with a quiet hum as the floor beneath her lifted for a second or two, then ground to a halt. She punched her apartment floor number again but nothing happened.

A chill crawled up Holly's spine. She'd never liked confined places. Was she trapped?

The man moved to the panel and poked a few numbers before he lifted his chin and glanced at the ceiling. "Hmm. Not sure what's going on."

Holly tried to breathe but only took in shallow gulps of air. Things like this happened on television -- not in the real world. A knot formed in her stomach. "Are we stuck?" She fought to control the rising tone of her voice.

The man's eyes sparkled as he gazed at her, then he looked about the small space. "Could be. Don't worry. We'll get out."

His assurances brought no relief. Holly's heart

pounded harder.

He fingered the panel, pushing the *Door Open,* and the *Door Closed* buttons a couple of times. Still nothing. "I think we better ring the alarm."

An alarm sounded in her head.

The three mirrors around the perimeter of her prison scoffed at her. She hadn't suffered from claustrophobia for a long time, not since the gruesome afternoon she lay bound to a gurney in the back of an ambulance.

"Oh dear God, I need to get out of here." She sank to the floor and drew her knees as close to her chest as she could. Her rocking motion did little to soothe her jangled nerves.

"Look." The big guy opened a metal compartment. "Here's the emergency call button. Relax. I'll get help."

She wrenched away from his kind eyes and hugged her knees tighter. The walls threatened to squeeze the life out of her. Gulping for air didn't help.

"Hello, hello. Can anyone hear me?"

The sound of clicking buttons drifted toward her.

The other occupant placed his mouth close to the panel. "Help! We're stuck in the elevator."

He settled back against the mirror appearing calm. His lips moved without a sound.

Holly pressed into the corner. Her reflection blurred.

"Hey, are you okay? Let me try something else." He punched another button and a shrill sound grated against her eardrums. The emergency alarm. Still nothing. The elevator was a dead thing suspended in space. She slumped against the wall as everything spun.

With a groan, the broad man bent down beside her and patted her arm. "I'm going to keep trying. But first, let me pray for us. It'll help." His warm hand caressed her shoulder. "Dear Lord, I trust You for our safety today. Please provide us with the way out of here. Until help arrives, I ask You to bring this lady peace. In Jesus name."

Her breath came easier, and she rubbed the pain in her leg. After standing all day, she'd only wanted to get home and rest.

Her companion hoisted himself up and poked his fingers into a small crack where the doors met. The gap widened two inches.

Some kind of metal tubes were visible beyond the double doors. The car was between floors. Panic struck again. "Oh no, what if this thing falls? How many floors did we go up?"

"It couldn't be more than a couple. This is a newer elevator. I doubt it would go into a fall." The man pried at the door again. It opened another inch. "Hello. Can anyone hear me? We're stuck in here."

Holly tried to steady her intake of air, remembering his soothing prayer.

"Hello." A voice sounded from below.

Thank you, God. She stopped digging her nails into her good leg.

The man put his mouth to the opening. "Yes, hello. Can you hear me? We're stuck in the elevator."

"Craig Schackelford, the general manager here. I've notified the fire department. We'll get you out. Shouldn't be more than a few minutes."

"You can stop worrying now." The heavyset man looked down at her and smiled. "For a second, I was concerned about you. Are you okay?"

She gulped. "I... I think so."

He ran his hand along the opening between the two doors. "I'd suggest you look out, but all you're going to see are the hydraulic cylinders. Just breathe."

"Hey there. This is Craig again. The good news is they've begun working. It may be a while. Try to relax. I'm terribly sorry about this."

Holly drew in a breath and looked up at her fellow inmate still poking at the space between the doors. For the first time, she allowed herself to take in his appearance to discover what she'd found so intriguing at first glance. With golden brown hair and soft blue eyes, he had one of the most handsome faces she'd ever laid eyes on even with a roll of flesh framing his chin and a large stomach protruding from his tee shirt and warm-ups.

"Looks like we're going to be out of here in a bit, Holly." The man knelt beside her, then plopped down on the floor.

"How... how did you know my name?" Her eyes widened.

"It says Holly right there on your nametag, just below *The Happy Smile Center*." He grinned, a twinkle in his eye again. "I'm Jess Colton. Seventh floor."

His face expressed compassion, like he really cared. She slapped a hand over her mouth as a giggle escaped, a release from tension. A neighbor? If his clothing was any indication, like her, he probably had to stretch his budget to live at Rainier Regency. "Holly Harrison from the fifth floor."

"Nice to meet you, Holly, even under these circumstances. Hope you wouldn't pull all my teeth if I come down to the Happy Smile Center?"

"No." She laughed, part of the stress melting away.

"I'm a dental hygienist with Dr. Murphy. How about you? Where do you work?" He certainly wasn't dressed for his job in those sloppy clothes.

Sweat poured down his face. "I'm a systems analyst for Evergreen Technologies. We're based in downtown Seattle."

Wow, that sounded like an important job. "A systems analyst? I have no idea what that is." Holly glanced at their reflection in the mirror. She looked a wreck, but her leg sat in the right position.

"I don't think you want a full explanation now, but I plan, configure, and install computer applications for various companies."

"Are you off today?" While she may have misjudged him based on his clothing, he sure wasn't dressed to go downtown.

"No, I work at home. Just started about a month ago. Beats fighting the Seattle traffic."

"Not as nerve wracking, I'm sure. Oh, and thank you for reminding me to stay calm. The prayer helped."

He nodded as if he knew a secret. "You're welcome. If I didn't have the Lord to rely on, I'm not sure what I'd do."

"I agree, but sometimes I think..." She wouldn't go there. God saved her from her sins, and she prayed to the Lord, but deep down, she doubted it did any good. After all, her sister Diana said the past would always have a bearing on Holly's life.

Yet how could she have known? Those months during college changed everything.

She wrung her hands. Maybe getting stuck and dying in this elevator would be her final payment on those sins. *Oh, God. I'm so sorry.*

He patted her fingers, stilling them.

"Just so you know. I don't go to church anymore." Having Diana remind her of her wretchedness was enough. She didn't need to hear it from other people.

The elevator groaned and shifted with a jerk. Her heart slammed into her stomach. "Are we going to fall?" She grabbed Jess's arm and hid her face against his shoulder. "Dear Lord, please get us out of here safely." She tightened her grip on the stranger as the elevator jerked again. Maybe Jess could convince God to save them. "Look, if we get out of here, I'll attend church once. Tell God for me."

Jess chuckled. "Will do." He lifted his gaze to the ceiling. "Lord, Holly says she'll go to church if You'll see us out of here." He held her at arm's length. "Okay, I think He heard that. We're fine."

"I'm being childish." Warmth climbed up her neck and into her face.

"I don't think so," he whispered.

The elevator wrenched, and Holly shrieked.

Jess put a finger to his ear and shook his head, but the knowing smile never left his handsome face.

Oh, finally. The cab moved downward, and the doors slid open. Never had she been so glad to see Mr. Schackelford.

Jess struggled to his feet, wheezing for breath as he held out his hand to her.

She clasped it and managed to stand. He was her hero -- he and the repairman. She straightened her slacks and stepped out into the lobby.

Mr. Schackelford bit his lip. "Ma'am, I'm so sorry. Please accept my apology for the delay." He ran a hand through his hair. "If I may, I'd like to offer you both dinner on the Rainier Regency at any restaurant of your choice."

Holly waved him off and headed down the hall. "Thank you, but another day. Right now I'm going to my apartment. I just need to relax."

Jess probably couldn't follow her up five floors at his size, but then, it wouldn't be easy for her either.

He chatted with Mr. Schackelford but looked up and smiled at her as she opened the door to the stairwell. If she could get away, maybe he'd forget about her promise to attend church.

~

Work was a nice distraction from the claustrophobic thoughts crowding Holly's memory since yesterday's incident in the elevator. Still, she welcomed Friday afternoon, the end of her week.

"I'm almost finished with the last step, Mrs. Blaine. Your teeth will be sparkling after I polish them." She dipped the brush into the cup of cinnamon paste and applied the powder as she glided the instrument along the front surface of the woman's enamel. "You can rinse in a moment."

What would she do this weekend? Maybe she'd call Diana and see what she and Red had planned, but knowing her sister and husband, they were probably either balancing the books at Sound Fitness or devising some new weightlifting class. They never took a break.

"There. You're done." Holly gave the woman a cup of water and pushed the receptacle of whirling water in front of her mouth so she could rinse.

Mrs. Blaine patted her lips with the green paper bib.

"Thank you. As usual, you did a wonderful job."

"I'm afraid not everyone is as devoted to keeping up their dental home care. You're my star patient." Holly unhooked the chain attached to the bib.

The receptionist stuck her head into the cubicle. "Are you free, *hija*? You've got a phone call." Marcela always called her "daughter" in her Spanish tongue.

"Yes, thanks, Marcela. Be there in just a minute." Probably a dental products salesman.

Holly waved good-bye to her patient and replaced her polishing tool. Then she tossed the disposable brush, quickly sanitized the equipment, and followed Marcela to the front.

"Here you go." Her friend pointed to the phone at the empty desk near the wall.

She picked up the receiver and punched the button with the blinking light. "This is Holly Harrison."

"Holly, Jess Colton. I apologize for calling you at work, but I didn't get your number yesterday. I wanted to know if you'd like to go to church with me Sunday."

She stiffened -- never dreamed he'd follow up with her. "Oh... maybe I'll pass this time."

Silence stretched between them for a moment, then he snickered. " Remember? You made a promise to God."

"I did?" She cleared her throat. Of course, and Jess hadn't forgotten as she'd hoped he would. "Yes, I did."

What choice did she have? She couldn't add a broken promise to her list of things God could hold against her. "Okay."

"Great. You want to meet in the lobby?"

"Oh, all right." How did she let this guy talk her into going to church? Jess seemed nice enough, but why was he so insistent?

She rubbed her forehead. Learning to forgive herself was first on her list. Learning to trust people again was the next.

~

Even in his dreams, Jess Colton never imagined he'd have a woman as pretty as Holly Harrison sitting beside him in his car. Her green eyes and light brown hair caught his attention the first time he saw her, the day she stepped into the elevator. The sprinkling of freckles over her nose gave her a childlike look, but he guessed she was close to his age, early thirties.

"I'm glad you decided to go today. Woodlyn Fellowship is a small, friendly church. I promise the people don't bite."

Holly hadn't stopped fiddling with the tissue in her hands the entire way from the apartment complex. Was she nervous around him, or ill at ease about attending church?

"Yeah, well, I suppose a promise is a promise."

"You said you used to go to church?"

She turned the tissue over in her hands then stuffed it into her opened purse. "Yeah." She swallowed hard. "It's not easy for me to talk about."

"Okay, but I'm a good listener when you get ready." The tense look on the woman's face tugged at his heart. What could have happened to keep her from church?

She opened and closed the clasp on her purse. "I don't think I'll ever be ready."

He gave her a wide grin. "The offer stands, just in case."

Holly cleared her throat as she chewed on the nail of her little finger. "Thanks."

Jess parked the car in the lot nearest Lake Wycot. The crystal waters next to a stand of Douglas firs always blessed him through the picture window over the altar.

He lumbered around and opened the door for his reluctant companion. The cool rainy season of Western Washington had given way to the more sunny days of late June.

She swung her legs out, tugged down on her pants leg before standing, and gazed straight ahead. Did the little building with its white vinyl siding and gray roof threaten her? He grasped her elbow and nudged her toward the door.

Joe and Connie Tyler stood on the threshold.

Jess leaned close to her ear. "Watch out. Here comes the attack of the friendly greeters."

"Good morning and welcome to Woodlyn Fellowship." Joe passed a bulletin to Holly, then one to him.

Connie spread her arms and engulfed them in a hug. Not an easy task.

Jess backed away and tugged his blazer to cover his big stomach. "Joe and Connie, this is Holly Harrison."

She held out her hand to the Tylers and smiled. He had to give them credit. They got her to loosen up when he couldn't.

His usual seat with more room waited at the end of the aisle toward the back. The feeling of being trapped between two people didn't appeal to him.

A hush came over the congregation when Pastor Downing's wife began the organ prelude.

The choir director announced, "What a Friend We Have in Jesus," and he stole a look at Holly. Her lips moved part of the time. But when they sang, "Oh what needless pain we bear," she slumped forward and twirled a strand of hair.

Pastor Downing rose from his chair and stood at the pulpit, the lake visible behind his thin frame. Jess couldn't remember a Sunday when he wasn't blessed by the man's power-packed message. "My beloved, I want you to understand who you are in Christ."

Holly fingered a tissue again.

"Satan would have you believe you are of no value, but the Lord says you were bought with a price, and you belong to God."

Jess's new acquaintance crossed and uncrossed her legs. She rummaged through her purse before setting it down on the pew.

"God is patient and slow to anger. You have been chosen by Him. Your relationship with Him is not based on yourself or anything you've done, but the work He did for you on the cross.

Now she picked up a hymnal and flipped through the pages.

"Believe me when I say you are free from condemnation. God loves you that much, my beloved."

Finally she grew still, her gaze glued on Pastor Downing. His words must've struck a chord. Her hands lay quietly in her lap as she stared at the preacher.

"You may approach God with freedom and confidence. Hope is only found in the Lord. Our regret or grief should turn us toward Him, not away from His presence."

She glanced at Jess then looked toward the front, a

furrow on her forehead. Did the pastor say something that touched her?

With a punishing thought, Jess froze. Maybe her unease wasn't about church after all. Maybe it was about sitting next to him. The fattest man in the building.

Chapter Two

Jess scooped up a large serving of mashed potatoes and plunked them next to the roast turkey, the fresh-off-the-cob corn, and the wheat roll leaving no more room on his plate. He drizzled brown gravy on top of the potatoes and turkey. In his other hand he carried a bowl of green salad with ranch dressing. The fried okra, baked chicken, and cherry cobbler with ice cream called to him, but he'd refrain today.

Holly followed him to the booth near the window with her meager selections, a single slice of roast beef, a few boiled potatoes, and some green beans. If he dined alone at Hometown Buffet, he'd make seven or eight visits to the line but not with Holly here.

She surprised him when she agreed to go to lunch. Even though it meant eating lighter, he wouldn't turn down the chance to share a meal with her.

She set her plate opposite his and slid into the booth. "Thanks for inviting me."

Jess sank onto the seat. "You're welcome. Mind if I say grace?"

She bowed her head and closed her eyes.

He slipped his hand over hers. Hmm. Was that his heart beating a little harder? "Lord, please bless this food to our nourishment." Sometimes when he ate alone, he forgot to thank God. Maybe praying would remind him to eat more sensibly.

She lifted her gaze and took a dainty bite. What was she thinking? The taunt lines on her face softened, and the stiff posture she'd held at church disappeared. Could he ask about her reaction to the message without making her uncomfortable again?

He swallowed a bite of turkey. "So, what did you think about the sermon?" Nothing like the direct approach.

The baby in the booth behind yowled. Yearning flickered in her eyes when she studied the child in the carrier. She wiggled her fingers at the infant before turning to Jess, but sadness lingered in her face despite the upward turn of her lips. "I see what you mean about a friendly congregation."

She'd avoided his question. Maybe her unease during the service wasn't because of his weight. After all she hadn't refuse his lunch invitation.

"Pastor Downing's been at Woodlyn for the six years I've attended. He gives some good sermons. Sometimes it's almost as if he spied on me during the week." Jess took a few bites of salad as he eyed the buffet line. A server put out some fresh rolls, probably soft and warm.

Holly dabbed her napkin to her mouth, took a sip of tea, and nodded. "I've felt like that in the past."

Jess peered out the window. She'd tell him in her own timing. No use in fishing for more information and making her jittery.

Barely eating anything, she pushed her food about her plate then took a small bite of carrots. "What he said made a lot of sense." She set her fork down and laced her fingers in front of her. "Like about how our problems should turn us to God and not away from Him."

"It's comforting to know He accepts us like we are."

She rubbed her neck and frowned. "How long have you lived at Rainier Regency?"

His dinner guest couldn't be more obvious. Church wasn't something she wanted to discuss. He wiped his mouth. "Wow, let's see how long it's been. Five, six years."

She turned her head back to the child at the booth behind them.

"Would you like to go for seconds?" Another run through the line would fill him up a little more, but he'd better not look like a pig.

For a long second, Holly stared at the child before she pushed her plate to one side. "That chocolate cake is calling to me. Do you want some?"

"I'm going to pass." If he ate one piece, he'd crave another.

Holly returned with a chunk of gooey chocolate cake and creamy icing on top.

He licked his lips. If he could just resist this once. Ludicrous. Who was he kidding? "Okay, I surrender. Back in a minute."

Jess picked out the largest slice left and shoveled it onto a dessert plate. Most of the time he'd go for two pieces this size and a bowl of ice cream. But today he'd compromise. Saliva seeped into his mouth as he plodded back to the table.

Holly had eaten a few bites of cake. Would she leave anything on her plate? Maybe he'd help her finish it off. So much for his concession.

His musings about food led him to Mr. Schackelford's offer. "I'm not sure if you heard, but Craig said we could go to dinner -- on him. What do you think? What's your favorite restaurant in the area?"

Holly's eyes lit up. "The Space Needle is always my first choice."

"Maybe we could go next weekend."

"Yeah, sure. We'll see." She left her fork on the plate by her half eaten cake.

Jess lapped up the last chocolate crumb on his. Though he loved every minute of being with her, the thought of the uneaten food on the buffet made him miserable. He'd consumed enough. In fact, he was no longer hungry, but he wanted to sample all the dishes he'd missed.

Only one answer -- return later in the day and eat everything he wanted.

~

Holly patted her full stomach as Jess maneuvered his car onto the circular drive in front of the apartment building's awning. She stepped out and walked around toward the entrance. "Thanks for lunch."

He leaned through the open window and smiled. "You're welcome. Guess I better get going. I promised my parents I'd drive up to Greenwood for a visit." He waved before he steered around the other side of the driveway.

She headed for the elevators, barely building up the courage to ride it. The jaws of the machine clamped shut mere seconds after she stepped inside. Since the incident three days ago, fear gripped her heart every time she rode up, and it didn't stop until she breathed fresh air outside the metal box. Walking up five flights of stairs again -- out of the question. The afternoon the elevator got stuck, she scarcely made it to her floor, and her leg hurt for hours afterward.

The elevator climbed upward. At least Jess's parents lived nearby. She had no one. Thoughts of her mother and their little house on the other side of Woodlyn drifted into her mind, the place where'd she'd grown up until her father's death.

Nothing could've stopped her dad from getting on his motorcycle that day. He wouldn't have listened to a girl of thirteen.

She'd always regretted Mom decided to marry Victor Kessinger five years later. Since the marriage only lasted six months, she didn't blame her for swearing off men and moving to New York State. Though Mom told her Woodlyn held too many memories, she still wished her mother had stayed around when Holly went to college.

And a couple of years after that, no one would've been able to keep her from making the same mistake as Dad. Those horrid machines had taken enough from her.

Ding. The light above stopped on *five*, and the doors opened. Relieved to be out, she strolled down the length of the familiar hall with the gold and black carpet.

Two years ago, who would've dreamed she'd live at Rainier Regency, one of the most exclusive apartment complexes in Woodlyn, though now she had to watch her budget every month. Her salary as a dental hygienist was adequate, but she wasn't getting rich.

Holly dug in her faux-leather purse and pulled out the keychain with the brass disc, "Hoh Rainforest" engraved on the front. She stuck the key in the lock, stepped into her air-conditioned apartment, and set her purse on the small table in the hall. The sofa in the living room invited her to sit down. Anytime she could get off her feet, she would.

Holly sank onto the off-white couch with its textured fabric and propped her legs up on the oak coffee table. She fingered the keychain in her hand.

The Hoh Rain Forest. She and Zack used to hike the trails under the canopy of the old growth trees, past nurse logs, ferns, and green moss. They'd leave the university, their classes, and homework behind for a weekend alone. She shook her head. Thoughts of Zack turned her cold inside.

She pulled her legs from the coffee table and returned her keys to her purse. Not a good time to call her friend from work. Marcela was probably doing something with her husband. She'd see her tomorrow anyway and tell her all about Woodlyn Fellowship. Her co-worker would be happy to learn Holly finally gave in and went to church even if it wasn't with her.

She looked at her watch. Might as well settle down with the book Marcela had recommended. Something about drawing closer to God. Probably the same kind of message she heard in church today.

Pastor Downing's sermon about God's forgiveness tumbled into her mind. He said the Lord didn't look at her wrong deeds but on what Jesus did. Diana always told her she'd never be able to live down her past.

Holly could receive forgiveness from her Savior maybe, but forgiving herself was too much to ask.

Nothing could erase the evidence of the earlier time in her life. Nothing could change it.

She stretched her arms in front of her and picked up the book. Might as well get comfortable first. She dropped the paperback on the coffee table, strolled into her bedroom, and plopped on the side of the bed.

The process had become so familiar she could do it in her sleep. First she folded up the left pant of her slacks to mid-thigh before moving her hands down her leg to the top of her knee. When she felt the carbon fiber laminated device, she slipped her fingers into the casing to release the suction. It gave way and her prosthesis slipped to the floor.

Her crutches leaned against the wall. She placed them under her arms and on one leg, hobbled into the living room, eased down on the couch, and picked up her book allowing the crutches to rest against the sofa.

JUNE FOSTER

Chapter Three

Holly trudged down the hall toward her apartment. A grueling day. Seeing eight patients wore her out. And her leg hurt. A sigh escaped. It felt good to be home.

She slipped the key in the lock and shoved the heavy door open. When it slammed behind her, a chirp sounded from her purse. She rounded the corner to the kitchen, set her bag down on the counter, and poked her fingers in the outside pocket.

Uh oh. The caller ID said Diana Harkins. "Hi, Sis. How's it going?" She traipsed into the living room and plopped down on the couch.

"Holly, this is for your own good."

Whenever Diana uttered those words, a prickle would race down Holly's spine.

"I want you to go jogging with me. Now, don't you dare say no."

How could Diana always sound so chipper? Holly leaned her head back and closed her eyes. "I've had a hard day."

"That's all the more reason." Her younger sister exuded energy. She never seemed to rest, always on the move, always running. But from what?

Holly progressed to the next point on her mental list of excuses. "What if it rains again?"

"Will you quit? It's not going to rain. I'll meet you in front of the building in ten minutes. I'm almost there." Holly's cell switched to the main screen.

No use fighting her. Resigned, she changed into a pair of sweats and a tee shirt. She never wore shorts, didn't even own a pair. With skillful fingers from years of practice, she folded up the left leg, switched the everyday prosthesis with her running leg, and tied her tennis shoes. A ponytail holder would keep her hair out of her eyes.

Why did she allow her sister to talk her into this? Diana had always been overly concerned. She even said she feared Holly would become too sedentary. The fact Diana owned a fitness center and taught aerobics three times a week might have something to do with it.

Holly ambled down the hallway to the elevator. She punched *Lobby* on the panel. Maybe no one would see her in these old workout clothes. The day she'd been trapped in the elevator, Jess wore old sweats and a tee shirt, but she doubted he worked out.

She pictured the round, handsome man. He exuded tenderness a lot of men didn't possess. Nothing like Zack, the last person to see her with a left leg.

Holly cringed with every thought of him. She'd held on tight when he lost control of the motorcycle and ran into the ditch. He didn't have time to react before they clipped the metal post that severed her leg below her knee.

The scars of remorse twisted her stomach. Zack came to see her once in the hospital, but never called again. A girl with half a leg probably repulsed him.

The elevator dinged and the *L* light blinked on. The glass doors to the outside of the building glided open when she triggered the beam. As she'd expected, her well-toned sister waited under the awning at the entrance.

Holly smiled. "Is this your version of sibling rivalry? Torture me by making me run?" A sweatband held Diana's short brown hair out of her blue eyes.

"Don't be silly. You'd be a remorseful hermit if I didn't force you to get some exercise." Diana clasped her hands behind her back and stretched.

A hermit maybe, but remorseful? Only when Diana reminded Holly she was at fault for all that had happened. No use in rehashing the old argument. "Okay." She tagged behind Mrs. Picture-of-Health down the circular drive onto the path by the side of the building.

Oh great. Diana took her to the Evergreen Woodland Trail that led behind the apartment building and north through the city maybe ten miles. "How far are we going on this thing? It's entirely wilderness, you know."

"Quit complaining."

Holly followed Diana in a series of arm and leg stretches. What a joke. Her leg, constructed of man-made materials, didn't stretch too well. She couldn't complain though. Most of the time her running limb was comfortable, especially since it attached with a rubber liner.

Holly jogged after Diana down the path bordered with ferns and lofty Douglas firs so prevalent in western Washington. "I have to admit. I couldn't enjoy the clean woodsy air and the call of a finch sitting in my apartment."

"That's why I phoned. You need to get out more. Do new and different things."

Holly sped up to jog beside her sister. The path curved to the left, leaving the hard dirt trail for a moss-laden forest floor. The stress of her day melted away as she entered another world in the woods. Mud puddles produced by the early morning rain dotted the ground. Newly sprouted trees grew next to a nurse log. "I did try something new. I attended church last week, and I enjoyed it, too."

Diana slowed her pace. "You went to church? What were you thinking? That's not healthy, not with the amount of guilt that had to come with it."

Holly blinked her eyes. Diana wouldn't leave the past alone. After all, it was Holly's burden, not her sister's. She opened her mouth to protest.

Diana's mobile sang. She frowned as she put the phone to her ear. "Hello." The call didn't slow her down. "Yes, honey. Okay. I'm on my way." She stopped mid-trail, then jogged backwards. "Sorry, sweetie. I've got to go. Red took his car to the shop and needs me to pick him up. I'm afraid I have to desert you. Hey, let's do this again." She reversed course and ran back in the direction of the apartment.

"Thanks a lot." Diana probably picked up on Holly's sarcastic tone. Since she didn't care to jog alone, she turned around, too.

Diana was right. Holly did need to push herself more. No excuses. Her skill at using her prosthesis enabled her to run. Many athletes had the devices.

She picked up speed as the grandiose building came into view. Home free.

A turn-off through a couple of Douglas firs led to the apartment. The ground became bumpy with potholes, limbs, and rocks. She tripped on a shallow hole, landing face down in a mud puddle.

Pushing up to a standing position, she brushed off her sweats and swallowed the word she wanted to say. Brown, slimy goo caked her hands, tee shirt, and hair. How could she have done something so stupid? At least she hadn't been injured.

Too humiliated to run, she walked the rest of the way. Her shoes squished on the dirt path. The cut-off trail passed in front of the apartments, and she turned down the concrete driveway.

"Holly, is that you?"

Mortified, she cringed when she heard the voice. Who spotted her looking like this?

Jess shuffled toward her. "Aren't you a little old to be playing in the mud?"

"Right." She rolled her eyes. "Had a little accident jogging."

His gaze swept across her. "Well, I think you look charming." He put his hand over his mouth and made a strained sound. Was he stifling a chuckle?

"Oh, thanks a lot." She laughed. "You fall into a puddle and see if you look this good."

"Here, let me walk you up to your apartment. You might not want to get mud in the elevator." He pointed to her tennis shoes. "Take off those sneakers, and I'll shake em' to get rid of the dirt."

Holly tensed. He didn't know what he asked. No way she'd reveal her prosthesis. "I'd better leave them on."

"Okay, well, at least let me push elevator buttons

for you and open your door."

Jess's tender gaze warmed her. He supported her elbow as they entered the lobby. Mud covered her, and he called her charming. She didn't deserve his kindness. An unexpected giggle bubbled from her throat. He truly was an oversized knight in rumpled armor.

~

Jess's sympathy went out to Holly. She looked embarrassed, and he certainly knew how that felt. He sensed a warm affection developing in his heart for her but nothing romantic. No woman would want him at his size.

They trudged through the lobby toward the elevators making slow progress since she sported those mud-filled shoes.

Just looking into her eyes, he could see pain. Something in her past still troubled her. He prayed the Lord would open the doors to talk about her issue, whatever it was. After he pushed *Up*, they waited by a tall potted plant for the doors to open.

"How can someone let themselves get so big?"

His heart faltered at the woman's remarks coming from across the lobby. The harsh voice cackled. "Did you see him, Harriet? His stomach jiggles when he walks."

"I think he lives on my floor."

Jess cringed. Unless Holly was deaf, she heard the remarks.

The door opened, and Jess followed Holly inside.

"Shh, Harriet. He might hear you."

"I don't think so. He already got on."

The elevator lurched when Jess punched *Five*. He looked everywhere but at Holly. He couldn't argue with what the women said. He was an overweight monstrosity. They didn't have to say it aloud, though.

"Hey." Holly touched his hand. "It's okay."

He shook his head, clenching his teeth to stay the emotion caused by the concern in her beautiful green eyes.

She gave him a warm smile. "Don't let them bother you. There're always rude people in the world. I've learned that lesson well." She patted his shoulder.

The door slid open, and they stepped out onto the fifth floor. Holly plodded along beside him in her muddy sneakers as he lumbered down the hallway. She stopped at her apartment and gazed at him. "Really, Jess. Don't worry. You're a very thoughtful guy, and I'm glad I met you. I always try to see the person on the inside."

Yeah. She wouldn't want to look at who I am on the outside. He kicked his heel on the carpet and pinned a smile on his face. "Thanks. Let me have your key."

She handed it to him, and with a twist and a shake, he pulled it out of the open door and turned the knob.

"See you later." The sooner he got back to his apartment, the better.

Embarrassment turned to anger, flaming warmth from his neck to his face. He took the elevator up two more floors and restrained the urge to kick his couch once he arrived safely inside.

The kitchen was his next destination. Two large frozen pizzas, one pepperoni and the other sausage, were stowed in his freezer. Only one at a time would cook in the microwave. He chose the pepperoni first.

When it finished, he slid the sausage pizza in and sat down at the kitchen table to devour the pepperoni. By the time the bell dinged, he was ready for the sausage.

The second pizza disappeared. He poked his head in the freezer again. A gallon of triple chocolate chip moose track ice cream called him. He set the container on the table and dug around in the silverware drawer for a spoon, not a teaspoon but a tablespoon. He carried his treat and flicked on the TV. Before too long, the ice cream carton was empty. He pushed it aside and sighed. He kicked up his feet, rested them on the coffee table, and exhaled a long breath. Except for the sluggish feeling, he felt much, much better. The women's comments no longer stung.

Chapter Four

With his nose in the fridge, Jess stared at the contents. He yanked at the bottom drawer, and discovered carrots, cabbage, green onions, bell peppers, even zucchini still in the plastic bags. After last night's binge, he needed to do better. Dr. Van Zant warned he was pre-diabetic.

He looked down toward his sneakers and couldn't see them for his bulk. He grasped a chunk of flesh around his middle, too much for his hand to clasp. What did that tell him?

Disgust swept over him. If he could slice the flab off with a knife, he'd do it. Maybe he could skip dinner. What did the doctor say? Skipping meals wouldn't help.

Hey, a stir-fry. He had plenty of chicken in the freezer, but first he needed a pan. His oversized stomach weighed on his lungs, cutting off his breath as he reached into the bottom cabinet for the wok. Standing up straight made him dizzy. He grasped the edge of the counter until the feeling passed.

The cooking oil he found in the cabinet above the sink rolled around in the skillet when he poured it in. It was supposed to sizzle. He turned up the heat and dumped in the frozen chicken chunks then shot back a few steps when the pan spit hot oil at him, stinging his hand.

Splotches of the slippery stuff spotted the floor. The kitchen towel hung on a hook near the stove, so he grabbed it and reached down to mop it up. The odor of burning chicken alerted him. He swung the towel over his forearm, reached for the spatula on the counter, and leaned over to stir.

He smelled a strange aroma and at the same time, a searing pain moved along his arm. An orange glow consumed the fibers of the towel. He grabbed one end and hurled it in the sink. When he turned on the faucet, steam and the odor of burning cotton and hair invaded his nose. He placed his arm under the cool flow.

The sting intensified. Beneath his short sleeve shirt, the flame had singed his arm hair off, and a nasty red mark ran from his wrist halfway to his elbow.

He swiveled the knob to turn off the flame under the stir-fry. Cold water from the spout didn't help much. He ran to the bathroom cabinet to retrieve burn ointment. None in there. He'd read somewhere not to put butter on a burn so he wouldn't try that.

Only thing to do was drive to the drugstore. He wrapped a clean towel around his arm, snatched his keys off the coffee table, and headed out as the pain worsened.

Halfway down the hall, he put on the brakes. Maybe he could borrow some burn cream from Holly.

The elevator must be running slow. He tapped his toe and whistled a tune, anything to keep from thinking of the stinging pain. Finally, the doors slid open. He stepped into the car, and it drifted down two floors.

At Holly's door, he punched the small white button.

She wouldn't mind helping him out if she was home. Out of breath, he leaned against the wall for support.

The door edged open six inches, and she peeked out, the chain still attached. With a smile, she lifted the lock and swung the door wide. Even his raw burned skin didn't keep him from noticing how her jade blouse matched her vibrant green eyes.

Her gaze cut to the towel on his arm, and her eyes widened. "Jess, what happened?"

"I don't need to borrow a cup of sugar but some burn medicine would be nice if you have any. I tried to make stir-fry and fried my arm instead."

"Sure. Let me take a look at it." She stepped back.

Jess lumbered past the entry into the living room, the layout of her apartment similar to his. "I ran cool water on it."

She rounded the corner to her small kitchen. "Good. Sit down." Two hardback chairs sat at a wooden table. "I'll be right back."

Jess lowered himself down. What an airhead. Thanks to Holly, he didn't have to drive to the drugstore. No doubt she kept stuff like burn cream and gauze on hand.

Holly returned with a plastic box and set it on the table. She pumped a dab of soap and ran her hands under the sink water then sat across from him. Just looking at her made him feel better. With a gentle touch, she removed the towel, applied the burn cream, and loosely wrapped the area with self-adhering gauze.

Though she seemed like she performed first aid every day, the cream stung. "Ow, that hurts." He sucked in a breath.

"Don't be a baby." A teasing smile crossed her lips.

Some flowery fragrance filled his nostrils. He gave her a sheepish grin as his face burned. Was it from her admonition or his accelerated heart rate? "Don't you know most men are just overgrown boys?"

"I believe it." She laughed. "Keep this on until tomorrow morning. I'll give you the gauze and ointment, and you can repeat the process then."

He blew out a breath and shook his head. "I should know better than to try to make anything more complicated than a bowl of cereal. My success in the kitchen leaves little to be desired." But worse than poor culinary skills, he didn't know when to stop eating.

"I'm headed out. Can I pick up anything for you?"

"No. I guess I'll go back and clean up the mess." He wouldn't be content with a small hamburger she'd probably bring back, but he appreciated her gesture.

"Well, if you're sure." She tilted her head and gave him one of her warm smiles. "I hope the burn stops hurting pretty soon."

"I'll try not to complain." He cut his gaze to a framed picture sitting on the kitchen counter. Two barefoot teens stood on the grass, the sun shining on their faces. The one with short brown hair had her arm around the other, Holly.

She followed his gaze. "Oh, that's me before..." A frown appeared on her forehead.

"Before?" Jess narrowed his eyes.

Her shoulders fell as she continued to stare at the picture. "Before I went to college."

"Who's the other girl?"

"My sister, Diana." Holly twisted the top on the cream and stuffed it in a plastic bag.

Did she have a bad relationship with her? Was that

the reason for the longing he saw in her beautiful eyes? "Do you see her a lot?"

"I went jogging with her before I fell in the mud puddle yesterday." Holly's eye twitched. "I tend to avoid her. She's very opinionated."

"I take it you don't agree with her opinions." He adjusted the bandage on his arm.

"Yeah, like her beliefs about God. She thinks He doesn't always forgive us." Holly put the gauze and ointment in a plastic bag and zipped the top. "I know better, but it's hard to let go of my doubts." She thrust the bag at him. "Jess, you seem to get me talking about myself. Reliving painful things."

"Sorry, Holly." Maybe he'd better put a muzzle on his mouth.

"I'll admit I feel comfortable spouting off to you." She scooted her chair back and strolled into the living room. "I trust you're not going to judge me." The area had built-in cabinets similar to those in his apartment. She opened the bottom drawer closest to the floor, shuffled papers around, and drew out a pink book, a Bible.

"If I judged you, God would judge me in the same way." Jess hoisted himself up and followed her.

Her eyes gleamed. "Your pastor's words got me to thinking." She set the Bible on the coffee table. "I may start reading this again."

"Whew. I was afraid I've been too pushy."

"No." She stared at her shoes. "Not at all. I'm glad for the little bit of prompting you've done. I alienated myself from the Lord." She ran her hand down her arm. "This is a small step in the right direction."

Better not prod her with any more questions, but

how bad could her past be? He moved toward the door and opened it.

She followed him and paused in the entry, looking up to him with green eyes dotted with flecks of amber. "Please be careful the next time you get the urge to be a chef."

He headed out the door but stopped, turning back to her. "Holly?"

She grasped her purse from a table in the entry.

"Thank you." No woman had treated him so kindly before. Yeah, maybe his mom growing up. She used to baby him. But not a woman his own age.

"You're welcome," she said.

He curved in the direction of the elevator. His arm tingled with the memory of her soft hands applying the burn cream.

A muscle in his jaw twitched as heat filled his cheeks. He stepped out of the elevator onto the seventh floor. When he let himself into his apartment, the warmth turned to ice, and his stomach growled. He'd never seen the kitchen in such a mess -- a burned towel in the sink and raw chicken in the skillet. With shaking hands, he opened the freezer door and pulled out two frozen fried chicken dinners and half a chocolate cake.

~

"Jimmy, you've got to open wider for me." Holly couldn't get past the man's pinched lips.

He glared at her from the chair in her cubicle.

She hated the days when Dr. Murphy saw patients from Harvest Home. His generosity extended to people suffering from schizophrenia, depression, and paranoia.

While she understood his kindness, she couldn't remember a day when at least one had been accommodating. "If you cooperate, you can be out of here quicker." She pushed a smile into place.

Jimmy scrunched his face. "I don't like you."

Holly took a deep breath and counted down from ten.

"I said I don't like you." He folded his arms over his chest and sank down deeper into the chair, continuing to scowl at her.

She mimicked his angry look, crossing her own arms over her chest. "Well, I don't like you either, but you've got to open up for me to clean your teeth." She pushed his lip up with her latex-gloved index finger.

He opened his mouth and clamped down.

Excruciating hurt radiated along her finger and traveled up the back of her hand. "Jimmy, let go!" She tried to yank her painful finger away, but like a pit bull with its prey, he held firm, moving his head from side to side. "Let go of me!"

Dr. Murphy rushed up behind her. "Jimmy, open your mouth right now."

Like an obedient puppy, the Harvest Home resident released her, eyes downcast. "Yes sir."

"He paid no attention to me." Holly gripped her wrist and held her throbbing finger in the air.

Marcela poked her head into the workspace. "Everything okay?"

"Yeah. Dr. Murphy's got the patient under control now." Holly's voice caught as she squeezed back the tears.

Jimmy pressed his folded arms into his chest, a frown on his face.

"I'm so sorry, Holly. Here, let me fix your finger." Dr. Murphy pulled off her disposable latex. "The bite didn't break the skin through your glove. That's a relief." The doctor opened the cabinet next to her dental chair.

He cleaned the inflamed area with antiseptic, wrapped it in gauze, before securing the bandage with tape. "I'm not an MD, but I can still deal with a wound. Times like this, I'm glad I require my employees to be current on tetanus shots."

"That should be fine." She didn't want to come off looking like a wimp.

Dr. Murphy glanced down at Holly's patient. The mentally disabled man sat in the chair spinning his hands around. "I'm sending Jimmy back without his teeth cleaned. Harvest can bring him again in a week or two. Next time I'll take care of him." He looked back to her. "Now please, go home and take it easy." He rubbed his forehead. "In fact, take an extra day and come in Monday."

She raised her eyebrow. "Thank you. Are you sure? What about my appointments tomorrow?"

"You work with your hands, and your finger needs to rest. I've got a list of substitutes available who can come in."

"I hope you don't think I was negligent." Holly couldn't afford to lose her job. Besides, Dr. Murphy was a great boss.

"Of course not. I need for your finger to mend." He scratched his head. "I thought about sending you for an x-ray, but I think it's just bruised."

"Well, I'll take you up on the day off. See you Monday." Holly grabbed her purse from under the cabinet and waved good-bye to Marcela.

The closest elevator was down the hall next to the insurance office. A woman with a baby stroller waited. When the car arrived, Holly smiled, held her hand out, and stood back, allowing the woman to push the baby inside. Wrapped in a blue blanket, the little one snuggled in the buggy. Holly's heart melted at the sweet face, leaving emptiness inside. If not for her choices, she might know the joy of holding a child close. "He's adorable." She waved good-bye when mother and child exited on the third floor.

Her finger throbbed with each step away from the elevator and to her Honda. A few days at home should help.

She'd take advantage of her time off and delve into the Word. Jess's church, his prayers in the elevator, and the faith he'd talked about reminded her how much she loved the Lord. Surely, she'd resolve her guilt someday.

The parking space for 516 in the basement at Rainier Regency waited. Maybe a little sun would do her good. Instead of taking the elevator upstairs, she found the exit that opened to the apartment gardens. The cool fragrant air caressed her skin. She'd relax for a while.

The pebble sidewalk led to the quiet haven enclosed by evergreen hedges and adorned with thick bushes and planters of summer blossoms.

A soft breeze blew a strand of hair in her face as she continued down the path, leading around the boxwoods. The garden's double rocker squeaked. Maybe someone had the same idea.

The corners of her mouth lifted. Jess pushed his feet on the ground so the chair swayed back and forth. He stared straight ahead as he rubbed his forehead, apparently deep in thought.

"Hi Jess. Soaking up the sun?"

He glanced up. "Hey, Holly, sit down. I'm enjoying this gorgeous Indian-summer day." He patted the space next to him. "To tell you the truth, I started wrestling with my computer early this morning. I figured I needed a quick break."

Even when he scooted over to the end of the long bench, it barely left enough room for her. His soft thighs wedged against hers.

She inhaled a deep breath and attempted to ignore her aching finger. "I know you explained it the day we got trapped in the elevator, but I still don't understand what you do."

"My work's hard to understand if you're not familiar with it, but I start by investigating and analyzing information for a company. I customize software to meet the client's needs. On occasion I follow up with extensive onsite training." He scrunched toward the other side a bit giving her a little more room.

"I'm not asking you any more questions. That sounds too complicated." She giggled at the serious look on his face.

His features softened. "I don't think I'd be too adept at cleaning teeth either." He gave the swing a push.

She touched his skin above the gauze. "I see you still have your arm wrapped up. How's your burn?"

"It's okay. You saved my life with your nursing skills. What about your day?"

He gave the swing another push, and she drew her feet up holding her legs straight out, careful to make sure her pant leg didn't ride up and reveal her prosthesis.

"Don't even ask."

His gorgeous eyes shone. As his lips parted in a smile, a tingle radiated down her spine, and she caught her breath. She had to admit she liked the way she felt when Jess looked at her. Was she attracted to the big guy?

The whistle of the five o'clock train wailed in the distance. When she told him about the problem she had with Jimmy, she experienced it all over again. "I'm so angry at the patient I could punch him."

Jess slid his arm on the back of the swing. "My shoulder's wide enough to cry on if you need it."

She exhaled a deep breath, smiled, and leaned back, nestling her head against his arm. The woody scent of his aftershave drifted toward her. "I'm not going to cry, but I'll rest for a minute."

"Help yourself." His peaceful voice calmed her.

She let out a deep sigh placing her bandaged finger in her lap. Her heavy eyelids closed. The warmth of the sun relaxed her, and Jess's soft rhythmical breathing lulled her senses.

He whispered. "Lord, I pray for Holly. Soothe her nerves and heal..."

The twilight of sleep wrapped around her as she faded into a land of dreams. Jess, the warm, sweet man, was with her. If she could only feel his arms around her, she'd be secure in them. He was so near now, his lips almost touching hers. She reached for him, inviting his kiss.

The haze of sleep lifted. Her eyes fluttered when his mouth found hers. Was this part of her dream? No, his rough cheek brushed her skin as his lips lingered.

"Wake up, Snow White."

The tender kiss quickened her pulse as she lifted her heavy eyes. "Snow White?"

"Well, you've been asleep for fifteen minutes. I figured it was about time you woke up. If the handsome prince could wake Snow White with a kiss, so could I. Although in this case, the prince isn't handsome, but Snow White is lovely." He gazed down at her.

Holly sat up. "Oh, I'm sorry, Jess. I didn't mean to fall asleep. Your arm must be numb." She memorized the gentle look on his face, and her heart skipped a beat.

"Yeah, it was a rough job, my arm around an attractive woman. I had to listen to the birds and enjoy the fresh air. Are you feeling better?"

"Much." Even her finger didn't throb like before. The nap relaxed her, but what did he think of her falling asleep on his shoulder? A wide smile filled his face. He didn't seem bothered. He'd even kissed her, but she'd encouraged it, pulled him near in her sleep. Had he really called her lovely?

"Come on. I'll walk you back to your apartment." He groaned as he pushed himself up from the swing.

They found their way around easy chairs, planters, and residents headed for the mailboxes, free of intruding gossips this time. The car propelled to the fifth floor, and Jess followed her out. He took the key from her hand and opened the lock, then stopped just inside. "I hope your finger feels better. Before I forget, my mom's having an early family dinner tomorrow. Since you're not going to work, why don't you drive with me up to Greenwood? My sister Margaret and her family will be there."

Was he asking her out on a date? Of course not. It

was merely a family event. "I think I'd like that."

Jess turned to leave. "Oh, give me your cell number, and I'll call you before I head down there, probably around three tomorrow."

She pulled a piece of paper out of her purse and scribbled her number. "Can I bring anything?"

The glimmer in his eye tripped her pulse. He lowered his voice to a whisper. "Just you."

Jess shuffled down the hall to the elevator, ample calves lumbering one step at a time. Before he reached the sliding doors, he turned his head back to her and winked. "See you, Snow White."

Holly smiled to herself. She closed the door inside her apartment and plopped down on her couch. Why had she dreamed about Jess, reaching out for him, during her short nap? His easygoing nature and warmth captivated her. Such a change from the last man in her life.

Zack only cared about himself. After he'd walked out on her, she'd never allowed another relationship with a guy. She couldn't risk the rejection again. Then, too, no guy would want her with her handicap -- and her past.

But Jess seemed different somehow. She could almost imagine he'd accept her as she was, unconditionally, if he ever fell in love with her.

She had to be honest. Jess Colton invoked romantic feelings in her heart. He was kind and affectionate. But would he still feel the same if he knew the truth?

She rested her head back on the couch and sighed. Nothing would ever come of their relationship. He must never know how she felt.

Chapter Five

The model Jess had drawn with a series of boxes and lines began to make him cross-eyed. A glance at his watch told him he'd better get ready. He started work at six every morning, yet he never seemed to get enough accomplished. His neck muscles complained, and he pushed up from the computer.

The half-full bag of chips and empty can of *queso* dip lay next to the monitor. He piled the stuff on the kitchen counter beside the open box of donuts with two left from the dozen.

The grungy cotton warm-ups and holey tee shirt landed on the bed in a heap. *Slacks and a polo shirt ought to do.* This wasn't an evening on the town -- just his parents' house in Greenwood.

Jess's heart had gone out to Holly when they sat in the swing, and she told him about the patient biting her finger. He'd watched her pretty face as she dozed. Long brown lashes resting on her cheeks sent his pulse racing. Then, she'd stirred and slipped her arms around him. Next, he found his lips on hers, and he could barely contain his beating heart. Surely she wasn't falling for him.

Maybe she'd dreamed about someone a lot thinner

and nicer looking. The kiss didn't mean anything. She'd think it all a joke since he teased her with the silly Snow White story. A striking woman like Holly wouldn't be attracted to him.

What about his feelings? Was he falling for her? His heart thundered in his chest even now. All right, he'd admit it. He felt something for her. So different from the drunken night he spent with Julie. With her it'd been sensual and fueled by alcohol, but Holly -- his attraction was something more. He respected her.

He flirted with danger since a relationship with a woman seemed unlikely. Maybe if he ever conquered his weight problem. But what were his chances there? His dieting failures piled up, counting calories, the carb diet, and even the "grapefruit before every meal" diet. Yet, what did he expect with the way he ate?

A laundered pair of slacks and a shirt still covered with plastic hung in the closet. He tugged them on and massaged his forehead. The suspicion his overeating had more to do with stress and the situation with Mom and Dad than an uncontrollable appetite plagued him lately. Could a human being really be so hungry as to gain all this weight? He shook his head. What did he need? A shrink?

With churning emotions, he slammed his fist into his palm and lifted his hand to his brow then closed his eyes. *Lord, You know how the weight started piling on when I gave up drinking to honor You.*

Jess rubbed two fingers over his chin. Not as smooth as he'd like. He headed to the bathroom and removed the plastic guard from his electric shaver. It buzzed as he knocked off the whiskers. With a little more force than normal, he whisked the toothbrush over his teeth. How could he, a follower of Jesus the Messiah, have slept with Julie, blatantly disobeying God? The alcohol masked his inhibitions. He gave it up after that but made a tradeoff -- food for booze. His shirt buttons strained over his wide stomach. The pants barely fastened.

One last time he ran a comb through his hair and remembered his promise to call Holly. He stuffed his hand in his pocket, pulled out his cell, and punched the speed-dial number he assigned her earlier today.

She answered on the third ring. "Hi, Jess. I'm ready." Her feminine voice snatched his breath away.

"See you in a minute."

The elevator descended two floors while he twirled his keys. His heart skipped a beat when the slender woman, her light brown hair braided, opened her door. Her welcoming look salved his insecurities. *Maybe she's happy to see me.*

A small ceramic pot filled with ivy rested in her hand. "This is for your mom."

"She'll like that." He smiled at Holly's thoughtful gesture.

The circular pattern of the carpet with its spheres in hues of gold caught his eye as he stared at the floor. He raised his gaze to the woman beside him, in awe she'd agreed to go with him.

"The traffic shouldn't be too bad this time of day." She straightened the belt on her rose-colored top. "Did you grow up in Greenwood?"

"Yeah. Since grade school." He stepped aside, allowing Holly to enter the elevator first and then punched *Basement*.

The lift jolted to a halt, and she floated out in front

of him. When she stepped into the parking garage, she limped for a few steps.

"Did you twist your ankle when you fell the other day?"

"What?" She gave him a curious stare. "Oh, no. I'm fine."

"My parking spot's over there." When they neared his BMW, he clicked the locks and opened the passenger door. Her fragrance swirled around him as she scooted in.

Squeezing into the driver's seat wasn't easy. He drove out to the main road. "How's your finger?" He glanced in her direction and back to the road.

"It feels better today." Her cheeks turned a soft pink. "I'm sorry I kept you from your work yesterday."

"Don't think anymore about it." He lowered the volume of a praise and worship CD. "I could've nudged you sooner." He dared another glimpse of her. "I know something else that's probably bothering you." Should he bring it up? He cleared his throat. "Our kiss." She probably felt self-conscious about it and wanted to forget it ever happened.

A sigh escaped from her.

He stared out the window not risking another look to see if her face went from pink to red.

"You read my mind. I was embarrassed by it. I didn't want you to think I was one of those brash women who make a practice of coming on to men."

"I don't think I'd ever believe that about you." Her response surprised him -- concern about what he thought.

He pulled on to I-5. A second later an annoyed driver zoomed around him, blaring his horn. *Impatient people.*

"I'm glad." Holly slipped on a pair of oversized sunglasses.

His tense shoulders relaxed. Good thing they'd brought the subject out in the open.

The sign indicated ten miles to Greenwood. He gripped the steering wheel. Asking Holly to dinner seemed like a good idea when they were a few more miles away from the dysfunction. "My folks can be a bit overwhelming, especially my dad." Apprehension jiggled his stomach. "My mom's fairly mellow, and Margaret's always mothering."

"I'm sure your family is no different than any other. You know how it is. You can choose your friends, but you're stuck with your family."

His laugh blended with hers. She was more easygoing now than the fearful woman he first met in the elevator.

"My dad thinks he's the best lawyer in Washington State." Jess took a deep breath. "Either you do things his way or you hit the road."

"Your childhood probably wasn't as chaotic as mine -- never knowing what kind of mood my mom would be in." She brushed a piece of lint off her white jeans.

"Oh, yeah, I know chaos. Dad's driven. He never relaxes. Sometimes I believe he began telling me what he expected when I was in kindergarten. Mom's completely opposite." He looked at the rearview mirror and changed lanes to pass. "She used to pick up after me all the time. I'm not kidding you. She treated me like a baby."

"I suppose a lot of moms are like that." Holly paused. Her gaze went to the front window. She blinked a few times as if fighting off emotion. "I don't know why families can't just get along."

A digital billboard advertised the local farmers' markets flashing pictures of veggies, fruit, and flowers. "My father and his brother are the worst. Some kind of competition going on there. I don't know why, though. Sometimes, I wished I'd grown up on Uncle Bill's farm with my cousin George. But Dad always said his brother held a grudge against us."

Holly blew out a breath. "Resentment is such a waste of time."

The interstate took them over the winding Lasish River before the landscape gave way to a section of wetlands. The familiar exit to his parents' neighborhood appeared. After he left the freeway, Hamburger Haven popped up on his right -- the place with the best cheeseburgers in town. He gripped the steering wheel to disguise his shaking hands. Holly would laugh at him if he told her he wanted to stop for a snack, but the thought of food comforted him. The anxious knot in the pit of his stomach would feel much better wrapped around a greasy hamburger and an extra large side of fries.

~

Holly wrung her hands as Jess pulled in front of an expansive two-story home in the upscale neighborhood. Obviously he had never lacked for anything as a child if his parents' home was any indication.

He held the door for her, and she swung her legs out, the ivy in one hand.

He'd mentioned the kiss in a nonchalant manner --

hadn't taken it seriously. What a relief. She had feelings for him, but he'd made it clear he didn't harbor any for her. He wouldn't have brought up the subject of the kiss in such a casual way if he did. Jess had too many other problems to worry about a relationship -- his work, a controlling father, and an apparent weight issue.

Yet, she was falling for this big hulk of a guy, the man God used to draw her back to Him. She'd rid herself of these blossoming feelings before they engulfed her.

A walkway led through a lush lawn to the landscaping surrounding the home. Hydrangea bushes and English lavender grew out of a ground cover of cedar bark. A well-dressed woman in her early sixties opened the door as they stepped up on the decorative concrete porch.

Jess reached toward his mother and kissed her cheek. "Mom, this is my friend Holly Harrison."

Mrs. Colton's smile welcomed her. "So glad you came." She stood to one side as she pushed the door open wider. "Come in. Let me introduce you to Margaret." They passed through an immense living room with a cathedral ceiling. A five-foot portrait of a man with features similar to Jess hung over the rock fireplace.

"That's my dad." Jess nudged Holly's elbow and pointed to the painting.

The picture dominated the entire room. She gawked at it a moment then glanced at Mrs. Colton. "I brought this for you." Holly held out the ceramic pot.

"Oh, how lovely. Thank you." She placed the pot on a side table and touched its leaves. "You're so kind."

Holly's gaze fell on the framed picture next to the

plant. Her breath caught at the sight of Jess under a tree dressed in hiking shorts and a tee shirt. His same pleasant smile brightened his handsome face.

She closed her gaping mouth. A healthy guy, his trim stomach flat above his shorts looked back at her. What had happened to cause him to balloon?

She tore her attention back to Mrs. Colton, following her through a gourmet kitchen and out a sliding glass door to a wooden deck. Flower boxes along one side contained lavender-blue periwinkles. A picnic table set for seven occupied the center of the cozy area.

A slender female version of Jess with the same striking blue eyes lounged in a green and white lawn chair.

"Margaret, meet Holly." Mrs. Colton beamed at her daughter.

Jess's sister studied Holly for a moment before extending a few fingers. "It's nice to see you. I understand you live in the same building as Jess."

Holly nodded and dropped her hold clasping her hands in front of her. She opened her mouth to reply.

Two teenage boys raced around the corner of the deck from a side yard. "Hey, Uncle Jess." One of the teens waved.

Margaret leaned back in her chair and propped up her feet. "This is Jess Edward and his friend Dale."

Holly smiled at the two active kids. "How ya doing, boys?"

They each gave her a shrug and dashed inside through the open glass doors. Teens had changed since she was younger. Though at times her mother didn't deserve it, and her stepfather never did, she always tried to respect adults.

Margaret tapped her cheek. "Those boys. What's a mom to do?"

Teach them some manners for one thing. Holly filled her lungs with a breath of air and pulled her lips into a polite smile.

"Oh, and Edward and Janelle went to her Girl Scouts father-daughter banquet."

The glass door slammed shut, and a trim man with graying hair surveyed the group as he stepped toward them. "Jess, who's your friend?"

Jess rubbed his chin. "Uh, hello Dad. This is Holly." He shifted his weight and fiddled with the buttons on his shirt.

Though she didn't feel like smiling, she forced the corners of her mouth up. "Jess tells me you're a lawyer, Mr. Colton. I haven't met too many in your profession."

"We're not all crooks as the standing joke would have you believe." He gave Holly an engaging grin but drew a piercing gaze to Jess. "Putting on a little more weight there, son."

Jess flinched. "Please, Dad, not now."

If she didn't clamp her mouth shut, she'd say something rude.

"Ah, just got to give you a hard time." Mr. Colton chuckled and slapped Jess on the back. "Don't worry. I've got another truckload of chicken to put on the grill."

Surely Mr. Colton wasn't so calloused as to think his words fell into the category of teasing. The lump in her stomach turned to rock. It took every ounce of restraint not to tell the man what she thought of him. Mr. Colton exhibited all the traits of a self-righteous donkey.

~

Jess wanted to disappear and find the hamburger shop. His father humiliated him in front of Holly. She'd never come to dinner with him again -- which might be a good thing.

He ate about half of the barbecued chicken on his plate, and even the potato salad didn't tempt his taste buds. And for him to pass up carrot cake was a marvel.

A pattern began to emerge -- he never over did it when dining with others, only when he ate alone. It would be too humiliating to allow anyone who knew him see his piggish behavior.

Holly didn't appear to mind when Mom dragged her off into the house to look at the family photo albums. Jess stepped down the stairs at the end of the deck and onto the expansive backyard. The narrow pebble path led to the old storage shed behind the wisteria shrubs. He leaned against the metal building, remembering the days of childhood when he used to have such fun in this yard, free of the encumbrance around him, the days when he'd been fit and athletic.

"I don't know why they had to name me Jess." The muted voice drifted from the other side of the shed. "I don't look anything like my fat uncle."

Jess's chest tightened, and he held his breath. Though a teen, his nephew's words pricked him.

"Why don't you go by your middle name?" Dale said.

"I try to get the kids at school to call me Ed."

Dale chuckled.

"Not funny," his nephew snapped. "How do you suppose he got so huge? If I was him, I'd just go on a diet. What's the big deal?"

"Yeah, I know what you mean."

"I'm embarrassed when I have to hang out with the dude." Jess Edward snickered.

"Bet he doesn't have any girlfriends. That pretty girl he brought with him today must be somebody he works with or something. Why would she like him anyway?"

Jess Edward laughed. "Who knows?"

Jess couldn't hear any more. His feet felt as heavy as his oversized stomach when he headed back to the house.

He didn't need to be reminded of a weight problem. Going on a diet seemed an easy solution, but time after time, he'd failed. Why try anymore? Maybe God had given up like he had.

On the deck, Dad cleaned the grill with a long handled brass brush. His gaze landed on Jess's middle. "Glad you could spare a few hours. How's your work going?"

"Fine. I'm designing a new application for Vauxhall Motors in Ellesmere, England. I've got a meeting with my boss in Seattle next week. Jim mentioned something about sending me to Hawaii to assist Regis Pineapple in setting up their software. He's going to let me know when I should plan on leaving." *Had he impressed his father?*

"That's great. Don't go to the luaus, though. It's easy to eat too much at those spreads." He closed the lid on the grill. "I guess you don't get much exercise sitting at the computer all day."

"Not much." Jess hung his head. No use arguing

with him. Jess had never been able to stand up to his father.

"Son, I'm going to tell you this for your own good. You need to do something about your weight. You've got your health to take care of, especially if you want to have a wife and family someday." Dad poked Jess's stomach. "Besides, what parent wants a tubby son?"

His father's words drove an arrow into him. Something else hurt even worse. His dad was right, no woman would want to marry him, but Jess didn't want to admit it -- even to himself.

Chapter Six

Holly crossed one leg over the other and tried not to dwell on the afternoon's events. She felt so sorry for Jess.

His white knuckles gripped the steering wheel. The silence in the car roared louder than the traffic on the interstate. He switched his radio on and punched another button which produced an easy listening station. Clearly he didn't want to converse. His jaw rose with the clenching of his teeth.

She turned down the volume on a Lionel Richie tune. "I really enjoyed the meal this evening. Your mom is so sweet."

"I notice you didn't say my father, as well."

Nor did she mention Margaret, but Holly wouldn't go there. "Jess, I--"

"No, I'm sorry, Holly. I shouldn't bring you into my family problems."

Holly wanted to reach out to the man whose father hurt him, but she kept her hands in her lap and her feelings in her chest.

The buildings in downtown Woodlyn materialized ahead. After Jess exited the freeway, he crossed two intersections and turned off toward Rainier Regency. In the parking garage, he cut the motor and strained toward her. "I doubt you'll ever want to go through that again, but thanks for coming with me this time."

"Please don't worry. I want to be your friend." She exhaled a deep breath. Hadn't he been a friend to her?

They exited the car into the parking garage. A stroll in the evening air would be perfect. "Let's walk out by the pool and cool off." Jess could *cool off* in more ways than one.

"Might as well." He punched the button for *Lobby*. When they passed the information desk, he held the glass-paneled door to the outside yard. A path wound around a group of poplars and a lilac bush to the adults-only pool.

The setting sun danced in elongated shafts of light across the crystal-clear water. The pool beckoned. A couple splashed each other in the shallow end, but never in her right mind would she go in. Very few people knew about her prosthesis. Regret squeezed her when she remembered the days she used to be a good swimmer. Oh, well. Jess probably wouldn't be caught in a bathing suit either.

She eased into a mesh lawn chair on the other side of the pool and propped her feet up. The other couple laughed as they got out of the water and toweled off. Hand in hand they walked toward the building.

Jess stared off toward the trees beyond the ornamental fence surrounding the pool. The outdoor chair barely supported him as he rubbed his temple.

What could she say to cheer him? "Thanks to your encouragement, I read some scriptures this morning. God says He looks upon the heart and not the outside of man. I see a kindhearted Christian guy when I look at you."

He jerked his head toward her. "Thanks, but I can't ignore the outside of me, you know." With a groan, he pushed up from the chair. Thumbs hooked in his pockets, he ambled toward the poplar grove. He bowed his head and stared at the ground, his back to her.

Holly shifted from her chair. Under Jess's broad shoulders, ripples of bulk were visible beneath his shirt. She brushed the back of his arm. "Something else I read. In Ephesians the Lord tells us we are God's workmanship."

Jess breathed a deep sigh and turned around to meet her gaze. "Yeah, well did He make me like this then?"

"I know things were tough on you this afternoon." She wanted to tell him about her problems, her past. Maybe it'd encourage him to know he wasn't the only one with troubles. But was now the right time? "I just need for you to know how special you are to me."

His gorgeous blue eyes studied her face, as if he didn't believe her.

"When I first met you, I thought I couldn't forgive myself. You encouraged me to think again."

Jess wrinkled his forehead. "What couldn't you forgive?"

Holly straightened. "I -- before I invited the Lord into my life, during my college years, I had a boyfriend. We spent a lot of time together." She swallowed. "I mean, nights and weekends."

"You're telling me you slept with him?"

She stared at her feet. "Yes."

"If you've asked God for forgiveness, He's granted it."

She nodded. "I know, and I believe that. I guess I

listen to my sister too much. She always tells me my actions continue to affect my life -- that the consequences don't go away. Diana thinks God will hold it against me from now on."

"She's right about the consequences. We create them. They linger, but Holly, God is the God of second chances."

"I just can't put what I did behind me. It's hard to forgive myself." She might be able to if the story ended there, but she couldn't reveal anymore.

He rubbed her shoulder. "We all do wrong. When we say we're sorry for our mistakes, God's gracious enough to forgive us." He ran his fingers down her arm and grasped her hand. "I don't think any less of you. If I did, I'd be a hypocrite. I'm glad you told me."

Giving into an impulse, she touched his prickly cheek, tracing a line down his face. "I need to tell you. You're valuable to God and to me, too." Caution and reason drifted away when she allowed her heart to take control. She wrapped her arms around his neck, savoring his nearness.

Then heat traveled to her chest. The sparkling pool became the focus of her gaze as she stepped back.

The soft, husky tone of his voice made her giddy. "Come here, Holly." Jess reached for her hand and drew her closer.

He slipped his arms around her waist, and she nestled her head against his cheek, hugging him again. Was this right? She wanted to avoid a serious relationship, but she couldn't refute her deep feelings for this man who loved God and reminded her she did too. But could he accept her if he knew the whole truth?

~

Jess struggled with his tie. He hated those things. Never could get them done properly. He checked his watch. If he didn't get out of his apartment in another few minutes, he'd miss his train. The Puget Sound Metro Rail Station's parking lot provided space where he could leave his car, but he needed to hurry to catch the eight-forty to Seattle.

The buttons on his gray lightweight summer jacket didn't reach. He left it open and lumbered out the door. A hot July day and he had to suffer in a suit coat.

Jess maneuvered the eight miles in the weekday morning traffic to the train station, yet this was easier than enduring downtown Seattle.

Since he'd begun working at home, he enjoyed the unhurried pace -- sipping his coffee instead of gulping it. *Time for a bigger breakfast.* But not this morning. His stomach protested this break in routine.

He entered the station's parking lot, pulled into an empty space, and plodded toward the main building. The double glass doors opened leading to the tracks. He switched his briefcase to the other hand and reached into his wallet to find a five dollar bill. The scowling woman behind the window passed him a ticket and his change through the small opening in the glass.

Commuters pushed through the turnstiles ahead. He stuck his ticket in the slot. *Click.* The bar didn't move. His girth had him trapped. He pushed again. The turnstile didn't shift a centimeter.

Sweat beaded his forehead. He jostled the bar harder and looked both ways. The handicapped entrance would've accommodated him.

He gave one more shove. Nothing. The bar behind poked him, but his hips, trapped in the side barriers, didn't budge.

"Hurry up, buddy. We're going to miss the train." Didn't the guy behind him see he was stuck? The beaded sweat turned into a river, pouring off his forehead. He breathed hard.

Men weren't supposed to cry, but his eyes stung. What could he do?

The guy behind him gave him a hard shove on his backside and the wheels turned. Jess lurched out of his confinement and glanced at the man with blond wavy hair and a muscular build.

"Thanks, guy." Jess waved at the man sailing by. Though humiliation inundated him, he was still grateful.

The train to Seattle arrived, and boarding passengers stepped up into the car through the sliding doors. His legs couldn't move any faster.

As a youth, he occasionally dreamed he ran from someone, but the ground was covered with mud. He maneuvered through the deep substance in slow motion. Now the dream became a reality. The sliding doors closed as he barely squeezed inside. He flinched when he thought about the turnstiles. His dignity had taken a blow.

A glance around the interior of the car revealed only one place to sit, a small area at the end of a seat for three. No way could he park himself in such a small space. He'd better stand, but his legs ached as they worked overtime balancing his weight. A teenage boy on one side and the blond man on the other jostled against him with every movement.

The metro made a stop at Ferndale and two women got off. Since no one else seemed to need the seat, he sat. Relief swept over him. He'd struggled to juggle his briefcase and hold on to the railing with one hand for more than a half hour.

He leaned back and gazed out the window. Mt. Rainier rose before him in the distance. At least the top portion. A shroud of clouds covered the lower elevations of the cone-shaped mountain.

Holly slipped into his thoughts. She'd blessed him with scriptures. In the same way God had crafted Mt. Rainer, Jess was His workmanship. *Am I really important to God?* The verses had fed his spirit, and he'd heard them from a beautiful woman.

Her nearness made his pulse race, yes, but there was something more. He yearned for her affection, and she filled him with joy.

Then his heart dropped to his feet. He couldn't love a woman or have a meaningful relationship. At his size, what kind of husband could he be to her?

Jess struggled to walk the three blocks from the train station to the Everett Building. Men and women in business attire, others in polyester vests and jeans whizzed past him. He turned the corner at Starbucks and lumbered down the block to the front door of the twelve-story building. The elevator on his left took him to the ninth floor and Evergreen Technologies.

"Hi, Jess." Patricia's pleasant smile greeted him.

He'd always liked their receptionist.

"How are things going at home? Miss you around here." She stuck a pencil behind her ear.

"Going good. Miss you, too, Pat. Jim's expecting me." He switched his briefcase to his other hand.

"Yeah, he's in his office. Go on in." She picked up the ringing phone.

He turned to the right at Pat's desk and plodded down the hall. At Jim's open office door, he tapped.

"Come in." The fifty-year-old man with a slight paunch smiled beneath a bushy mustache and rose from behind the mahogany desk to shake his hand. "Thanks for making the trip downtown. I know you're getting spoiled working at home."

"It's nice not to have to commute everyday like I used to." Jess grinned at his boss. "So what's up?"

"Sit down, Jess. Sit down." Jim eased back into his seat.

Jess lowered himself into the large brown leather chair in front of the desk and set his briefcase on the floor.

A frown flicked across Jim's face for a moment and then he smiled.

"As you know, we need to send someone to Oahu to set up the Regis Pineapple software system you developed. I'd mentioned sending you." He cleared his throat. "Just wanted to let you know we've decided to send William Oatman instead. I can't take you off your current project. It's too important."

Jim lowered his voice and leaned forward. "Besides, he's going to have to take some employees scuba diving. It's expected over there in Hawaii. He'll also have to wine and dine 'em. I figured you wouldn't be interested in scuba diving." His laugh was a little too loud.

"Sure, Jim. I understand." *Why'd he ask me to come all the way downtown? You'd think breaking this kind of news would've been easier over the phone or in an e-*

mail. After the harrowing trip into town, he'd rather not make the long journey to Hawaii anyway.

As if reading his thoughts, Jim opened his mouth. "There's something else, Jess. I need to touch base with you. Mr. Zimmerman held a meeting the other day and spoke to me about your project. Upper management needs progress to move along a little faster. Is your home situation working out for you?"

"Yeah, it's fine." He worked nine hours a day, but maybe he'd better up the hours. Of course, if he spent nine true hours at the computer rather than getting up and down to eat, he'd probably get much more accomplished.

"Hey, I'm not worried about it at all. You're the most highly-trained person we have. Just wanted to give you a little nudge."

"Okay, Jim. I'm on it." Jess rose to leave and stuck out his hand to shake his.

"One more thing. Mr. Zimmerman wanted me to talk to you in person and have you sign this counseling statement. I'm sorry. This wasn't my idea." Jim wiped his brow with his handkerchief and shoved a paper at Jess.

Jess's body became rigid. "What is it?"

"It states I've discussed the necessity of speeding up the progress of the project. Again, I'm sorry, but you know how the big boss can be."

Jess placed the paper on Jim's desk and signed. The document merely stated what he'd already said.

Jim tore the duplicate copies apart and gave one to him.

"Okay. I'll check with you in a few days. Take care." Jim turned his attention back to a pile of papers on his desk.

Like a zombie, Jess made his way back to the station for the return train to Woodlyn. He scanned the same two-way ticket, this time careful to go through the handicapped area.

His conversation with Jim pressed on him like the extra weight he carried. Obviously Jim and Mr. Zimmerman were dissatisfied with his progress.

His preoccupation with food had prevented him from finishing the job. Evergreen was sending William to Hawaii to train Regis Pineapple employees how to use an application Jess had developed. Why? Because William was younger, thinner, and better equipped to work and play with the people there. Imagine Jess going scuba diving. A big joke. Except he wasn't laughing. He squeezed his hands into fists. He couldn't fail at his current job.

The day before, his father had berated him about weight. Jess had used the trip as leverage, hoping to make his father proud of him. *What would Dad say now?*

His father. He'd always tried to please the man. In the past when Jess failed, he numbed the pain with alcohol. Too much alcohol.

Giving up drinking had been easy for him, especially after he learned how vulnerable losing his inhibitions could make him. Eating didn't do that. He was always in control of his faculties when he ate. Food comforted him -- a fix whenever life got too tough.

"Addiction." The word spoken aloud stung. He was addicted to eating with no way out.

Chapter Seven

Sunday morning. Jess punched Holly's speed-dial number. "Hey, you want to go to church with me?"

"Sure. When are you leaving?"

"I'll knock on your door in an hour."

He turned off his computer and headed to the bedroom, trying to avoid the conclusion he'd made the other day. No matter how much he wanted a body bursting with vitality, with every cell fed with nutritious food, he continued to binge on sweets and fatty snacks.

After he dressed, he looked at his watch, picked up his Bible, and headed out of the apartment door.

Since his trip to Seattle two weeks before, it became clearer -- he battled an usual foe -- food. He couldn't stop overeating. The other night, he'd actually had a war with a battalion of chocolate-covered cherries.

At the store, the box had jumped into his cart, but no worries. He'd share with Holly or one of the neighbors. *Right?*

At two in the morning, he heard the morsels calling to him. He snuck into the kitchen. By the time the battle was over, he'd sustained injuries, his body beaten and bloodied by sugar. Half the chocolates were in his stomach, a fourth in the garbage can, and a fourth back in the cabinet. No doubt he'd be rewarded for his efforts with more armor around his middle. Though he saw a bit of humor in the situation, in reality it was no joking matter.

Jim's words reverberated in his mind, one reason he'd lain awake in the middle of the night. *Be more productive. Move the project forward faster.* Since his meeting with his boss, he'd upped his hours to eleven. Some system analysts worked fifteen hours a day. He shouldn't complain, but were his efforts enough?

Jess pressed Holly's doorbell. When she opened the door, he held his breath. Her blue slacks and white lace blouse hugged her shape perfectly. "Hey, Holly." A teenager couldn't have felt more awkward. "You look sensational, and because you're dressed up in your Sunday best, you can't say no when I tell you we're going to Pepper's on Alki Beach after church. Their Sunday seafood brunch tops all the rest in Seattle."

"No." Holly shot him a wide grin. "Only kidding. But what about your parents? Aren't they expecting you?"

"I begged off today." *A needed break.* He gave her a playful tap on her shoulder. "If it's okay with you, we'll let Rainier Regency pick up the tab."

She pulled her apartment door closed. "Well, Craig did offer any restaurant in Seattle."

"You said the Space Needle was your favorite. I promise to take you there another time."

"That restaurant really is expensive." She lifted her purse's strap on her shoulder and clutched her Bible.

"I can handle it. Besides you're worth it." Finances weren't a problem for him, thank the Lord. Senior analysts in Washington made a generous salary, right at six figures, and he had no other mouths to feed like some of his colleagues. Even though he probably ate as much as a family of four.

He held the car's door for his pretty friend. A little wisp of hair fell away from her braid and her lips curved upward in a smile doing wonders for his disposition. A woman like Holly accompanying him to church -- amazing. He couldn't wait to hear God's Word with her in the pew beside him.

When they walked in, Jess led the way down the aisle and stepped back allowing Holly to ease into the pew first. He held his head high when he edged in next to her.

Joe and Connie turned and smiled at them. Then the old doubts niggled at him. Had he lost his heart to Holly? He was afraid the answer was yes though their relationship wasn't going anywhere. *Guess I'm just a guy full of foolish dreams.*

He shook his head. His musings pulled him in opposing directions. Wasn't God in control of his future? Chiding himself, he willed his thoughts back to the service.

When the worship team left the platform, Pastor Downing perched on his stool and pulled the lectern holding his notes and Bible closer. Jess resisted the urge to cover Holly's hand with his when she rested it on the pew between them. She turned her head to him with a warm smile when he changed his mind and laid his hand over hers.

"Before I begin the message, I'd like to announce the elders have chosen the new youth pastor from the list of candidates you approved. Thank you so much for your prayers in this process. Timothy Garrett should arrive in a month, around the first of September."

Pastor Downing looked at his notes and raised his head. "God loves and values each of us. Romans, chapter six, tells us our old self was crucified with Christ, and we are no longer slaves to sin."

Jess sat up straighter. Was he a slave? Slaves didn't have a choice in the matter. Time and time again, he felt compelled to overeat. Even though he wasn't hungry, he couldn't say no. Yet he always despised himself afterwards. Wasn't that what slavery was? Being forced to do something against your will? But who or what forced him?

What about sin? Was eating a sin? Of course not. Yet overeating was. The notion seeped into his head like water dribbling down between porous rocks.

He had almost closed his Bible the other morning before he read the passage in Proverbs. God gave a command in chapter twenty-three. "Do not join those who drink too much wine." The rest of the verse shocked him. "Do not gorge on meat." Which meant any kind of food. The psalmist warned not to overeat.

I gorge myself on a daily basis. Did he sin every time he ate? He wrenched his mind back to the message.

Pastor Downey thumbed through his Bible. "Don't you know your body is the temple of the Holy Spirit? Honor God with your body."

Okay, Lord. I'm getting the point. But guess what? I'm powerless to stop overindulging. I've tried.

Jess sank further down on the pew. He should never talk to God this way.

With his head bowed and his hands over his eyes,

he perceived a small still voice. *You're right where I need you to be.*

He shook his head. *God, I can't obey You. I can't live without food or go without my binges. It's the only thing keeping me sane.*

~

Holly loved the table Jess requested. They sat next to the glass divider on the wooden deck jutting out over the water. She filled her lungs with the salty air. The snow-capped mountains of Olympic National Park silhouetted the darker blue hills of Bainbridge Island.

The wrought-iron table supported a red and white umbrella. She turned her gaze from the blue waters of Elliott Bay to Jess. "That was a good sermon today. What do you think?"

"Yeah. Have you looked at the menu? Or would you rather have the buffet?" Jess sipped his iced tea.

Hmm. Was he avoiding her question? "I think I'll have the buffet. Can't pass up the garlic shrimp, Dungeness crab, lobster tails, and baked halibut."

Jess nodded, reached for her hand, and bowed his head. "Lord, thank You for this meal, and we ask you to bless it to our nourishment. Please remind me to pray every time I put food in my mouth. In Jesus name."

Holly trained her gaze toward the pained expression on his face. His prayer sounded like a plea for God's help.

The buffet tables filled the main dining room's serving area. The salads, carving stations and even the fresh prepared crepes with fruit compotes tempted her appetite.

With a plate filled with almost everything, she strolled back outside, Jess by her side. "The selection of seafood is incredible. We couldn't ask for a more glorious setting, either. It's a good thing Rainier is paying for this. My budget would've complained."

Jess took a bite of lobster quiche and glanced toward Puget Sound before looking back at her. "How am I so lucky to be sitting here with a woman who's not only beautiful but a Christian?"

Holly's heart pounded. She hated to think of the days before she found faith in Jesus and the years she'd turned her back on Him.

She'd paid an enormous price for her mistakes and could never erase the memory of the night in the hospital.

Thoughts of the days before the accident and before she'd become a Christian wouldn't stay buried. The world said if it felt right, do it. She had no conviction when Zack pressed her for more. She thought she loved him, but what did a young college student know?

Then a few weeks before the accident, she confirmed her fears with the pregnancy test. At a loss, she'd weighed the alternatives. Not that she'd ever consider aborting her child. There were other options. Keep the baby or give it up for adoption. Looking back, she knew she would've kept her child.

The day of the accident, though, she still hadn't made a decision and hadn't told Zack. Only six weeks pregnant, she wasn't concerned about getting on the back of his motorcycle.

Her carelessness cost her not only her leg, but something even more precious. She'd miscarried, losing her baby forever. She never told Zack about the loss, either. What was the point? Later, like all her other friends, he avoided her.

A hand covered hers. "Holly? Is the meal okay? You look like you're a thousand miles away." Jess's pale blue eyes swept over her face.

"It's wonderful." She smiled and squeezed his hand.

This morning the words Pastor Downing shared from Romans spoke to her. Despite her past, she'd been justified before God.

The sparkling waters of Elliot Bay enchanted her. A sailboat caught the wind and disappeared behind Bainbridge Island. But the man across the table pulled her attention from the blue sky and distant mountains.

His light brown hair was full and combed to the side with an errant strand on his forehead. When he looked at her, he made her feel like the only woman on earth. She cared about Jess -- heavy or not. She reached for his hand. "Jess, I need to tell you --"

"Holly." Diana waved as she made her way across the deck.

"What are you doing here?" Holly pulled her hand from Jess's. "This is my sister, Diana."

Jess stood. A gentlemanly thing to do. Not every guy practiced good manners. He stretched out his hand in greeting to Holly's sister. "Nice to meet you." He glanced behind her. "Can you join us?"

"Oh, no. I'm here with my husband. We saw you in the buffet line." She yanked her attention back to Holly. "I'm sorry I haven't been over to jog with you lately. Sound Fitness keeps me busy."

Diana's gaze ran the length and width of Jess. "I own a fitness center in downtown Woodlyn."

Jess looked at the floor. "That's great."

"We accept new clients all the time." Diana turned to Holly, raising her brows before returning her gawking stare to Jess. "Have you two been friends for long? Maybe you can bring Jess down to the gym. We can give him a workout, get him in shape."

Heat rose on Holly's face. Diana not only embarrassed her, she probably humiliated Jess. Her sister placed such an emphasis on fitness. Didn't she know the true person lay beneath the surface?

Her friend carried extra weight, but Diana's standards were different than hers. "Jess lives in the Rainier Regency two floors up from me. We met a couple of weeks ago, and we've become good friends."

"Oh, how nice. I can see you enjoy dining out." Diana waved her hand over their full plates, a sarcastic smile curving her lips.

Holly ignored the dig. "Jess is trained in computer science. He works designing software for his company." The words brought satisfaction. He had an impressive career, and Diana needed to know.

"Must not have opportunity to work out much. Jess, really, why don't you come down to my gym? We can work on some things for you." She gave him a wink.

"Diana, I'm sure Red's waiting for you." Holly punched her fork into a piece of shrimp. She'd love to forget her manners and stuff it into her sister's mouth.

"Oh, yes. Well, sit down, Jess. Don't want to wear you out." Diana turned and bounced back through the door to the main dining room.

Jess slumped back down in his chair. The pain on his face stung her.

"I'm so sorry." She reached for his hand. "I've never seen her quite that rude before. Sometimes she does stuff like that. Please forgive her."

He pushed his plate back and gazed out at the Sound. "It's all right. I get those remarks all the time." He brushed his hair off his forehead and smiled. "Do you have any more sisters?"

A laugh escaped her throat. "No, just the two of us. I think that's enough." She took a sip of her iced tea. "When my dad died, Mom didn't have any more after she remarried."

Diana strolled past a couple with fussy twins. Each parent taking turns cooing and cuddling the little bundles. Holly focused her attention on the children for a moment.

An ache swept through her. She pulled her gaze from the pink bonnet, catching sight of her sister, who also stared at the two small children. Then Diana tucked her sleek form close to her brawny husband and allowed him to lead her to the buffet.

Jess reached for her hand. "Holly, you were saying?"

"Oh, yes. Mom married Victor Kessinger. The second marriage didn't last long. The short time he was with us, he never loved us like a flesh and blood father would." She cleared her throat. "Diana always said we grew up in a dysfunctional family. I began to see it that way, too."

Jess smiled and raised his glass of tea to her. "Here's to dysfunction. Family life would be boring without it, don't you think?"

She clanked her glass with his. He was trying to make light of it. But he could do something about his weight. Nothing would bring back her child or her leg.

Jess wrote in the tip on his bill and lifted his credit card from the black plastic tray. He stuck the receipt in his pocket to give to Mr. Schackelford. How could such a sweet woman like Holly have a sister like Diana? Her insinuations and words still pricked.

But looking at this beautiful woman quieted the hurt. She wasn't ashamed of him, even defended him. Was there a way to extend the moment? "Let's go over to the beach before we drive home."

She didn't seem as happy as before the meal. "I'm not bothered by Diana. Don't let it worry you."

They left by way of the main dining room and emerged into the sunshine. Relief calmed him when they hadn't passed Diana's table.

Alki Beach lay just beyond Pepper's, a short walk. A visit to the waterfront would do them both some good.

Holly slipped her arm in his. "Not too many days of the year we can stroll on the beach with full sun."

The brick footway ran along the shore with stairs leading to the sand. A concrete bench rested on the sidewalk in front of the stairs. Holly plopped down. "A good place to watch the sunbathers and joggers." She patted the seat next to her.

Jess dropped down beside her. He could almost feel the sand between his toes.

"Let's take our shoes off and get our feet in the water." Jess removed one loafer and then his sock. He wiggled his toes in the air and smiled at Holly.

The horrified expression on her face baffled him. "Come on, girl, the water's not that cold. Get those sneakers off."

She stood, her eyes wide. "I -- I don't want to. Let's go."

He slid his shoe back on. "Well, okay. No big deal."

She trudged off toward his car parked to the side of Peppers. What could've upset her about wading in the water?

~

Holly took off her prosthesis and slid it down beside the couch. Saturday's mail -- she'd forgotten to check her box. Maybe she should go down and get it. But she'd taken her device off for the evening. The effort to put it back on wasn't worth it. She reached for her crutches. Would she have the nerve to use them in the lobby?

The crutches fit under her arms as she maneuvered toward the front door, hopping half the time. *Lord, I've got to come to a place where I don't always have to hide my condition.*

Jess had suggested she take off her shoes. He wanted her to feel the sand between her toes. No way he could've known she only had five.

The apartment key shifted in her jeans pocket. When she opened the front door, she rested her shoulder on it and took a step into the hall.

Movement on the right caught her eye. A neighbor reached down for a newspaper in front of his apartment. A cold chill ran along her spine. She backed into the entry allowing the door to close. Her nerve abandoned her. No one could see her like this.

She stumbled back to the couch and sank down,

parking her crutches on the floor. Would she ever be comfortable revealing her handicap to Jess?

Her pocket vibrated as her cell chirped. The caller ID said Diana. *Do I have to talk to her now?*

"Yes, Diana."

"Hi, Holly. Good seeing you today."

Well, it wasn't good seeing you.

"Who is this Jess guy?"

"I told you. He lives in the apartment building."

"Look, Holly. I usually don't interfere in your life."

Yeah, right.

"I was a little shocked when I saw you out with such an obese man. You can do better than that. Don't sell yourself short."

"You don't have a clue, do you?" Holly's blood pressure rose. "He's a wonderful Christian man, and I care about him, deeply. I don't need your approval." She clicked the *End* button, folded her arms in front of her, and fumed. Diana saw Jess's obesity. Holly saw his sweet humanity.

Chapter Eight

"Hey." Holly waved as she passed the receptionist's desk.

Marcela looked up with a smile.

"I'm meeting my sister Diana at Michael's for lunch. Back in an hour."

"Okay, *hija*. Don't eat too many enchiladas."

"Don't worry. They only serve soup, salad, and sandwiches." Holly raised her purse over her shoulder and took the elevator to the ground floor. The sliding glass doors led into the glorious sunlight. Even in downtown Woodlyn, the fragrance of evergreen trees filled the air.

September and the cooler temperatures would be here soon. She'd better enjoy her favorite season -- summer.

When Diana called and asked her to lunch, she probably felt a bit guilty after the way she behaved at Peppers. But Holly had to admit, she shouldn't have hung up on her either.

The upscale deli wasn't far from the Harbor Lights building. Not much of a walk. Holly crossed the street when the pedestrian light flashed green. In the next block, she passed Starbucks, a gift shop specializing in products from Washington State, and a children's clothing store.

She slowed to look in the window of the baby boutique. A pink doll house rested to one side with yellow and blue blocks in front. On the other end, a furry teddy bear sat beside a baby buggy. An infant mannequin adorned in a layette, including a frilly cap, tore at her heart. A large box of diapers sat to the side of the bear. Holly wiped a tear from her eye and trudged on to the deli.

Diana would probably be waiting for her since she could get off work whenever she wanted. Holly glanced through the large glass window. Sure enough, her sister sat at a table toward the back.

Holly hadn't realized she was hungry until she strolled past people eating sub sandwiches on whole wheat bread and Caesar salads.

Her sister waved and smiled. A beaded headband held back brown hair, all except the wispy bangs on her forehead. "Hi, Holly. I figured you wanted a salad, so I ordered you one and a glass of tea."

Typical Diana. Always in control. "Thanks. A salad would be great."

A server brought two tall glasses of tea with sprigs of mint floating on top.

Diana poured a packet of no calorie sweetener in her tea and stirred. "You sounded pretty upset over our conversation about your date." She didn't waste any time getting to the reason for the impromptu lunch. "I didn't mean to get you mad. You've been through enough. I should've been kinder."

Holly ripped the top from her sugar packet, dumped the contents into her drink and stirred, her spoon clinking against the glass. Diana still pitied her. "Jess is a great man -- a good friend." No way would she tell her about her real feelings for the guy. The woman seated behind Diana giggled and rubbed the arm of the man sitting with her.

"Does he know about things?" Diana raised an eyebrow.

Holly slapped her hand against the tabletop. "Yes, he does. Part of it."

"Well, you'd better tell him the whole story if you get serious about him."

The server brought two chef salads to the table, leaving the check. Holly bowed her head to pray, something she hadn't done much of in the past few years. When she looked up, her sister stared before stabbing a piece of lettuce and a small chunk of cheese.

Holly clenched her teeth. "There's something I wanted to talk to you about. I know I did a lot of stupid things in the past, but I've asked God's forgiveness." She sprinkled some pepper on her salad.

"Look." Diana lowered her voice. "You slept with Zack, and you weren't even married. Sleeping with somebody who's not your husband is wrong. God won't let you forget you broke His rules."

Diana held to Holly's sins almost as tightly as she had always done. "I made a mistake. Tell me. Why are my failures so important to you?"

"The least you could have done was marry him." Her sister fixed a piercing gaze on her. "That would've made up for it. I've talked to Zack recently. He's a nice guy."

Holly sighed and put the piece of bread she'd retrieved from the cloth-covered basket on her plate.

How had Diana found Zack? He'd walked out of Holly's life, and she had no idea where he'd gone. "He came to see me in the hospital once after the accident, and I never saw him again, but that's beside the point. The problem here is your questionable theology."

"What's worse, you got pregnant." Diana ignored her. "You weren't even thinking about the child when you rode on the motorcycle that day. After what happened to Daddy, I've never understood how you could've been so careless." She pressed her lips together. "I don't want to hash over the past again."

Holly took a deep breath and released it. "That suits me fine. I don't want to discuss my failures with you, either. I've turned them over to God."

"You slept with a man outside of marriage. You got pregnant by him, and let your baby die because of carelessness." Diana's smug voice pelted her. "And Holly, *you were* careless."

Holly's stomach lurched at the anger and self-righteousness in her sister's words. She raised a silencing hand and threw her napkin on the table. "Pay attention to me for once. I've listened to you long enough. I read in my Bible this morning--"

"Your Bible? You're reading a Bible?" Diana's face screwed into a snarl.

"Yes, in Psalm 130, I read about God's forgiveness. I know I've failed Him, but He's bigger than my weaknesses."

Holly waited for her sister to refute her. When Diana remained silent, she continued. "During that horrible time in my life, I didn't even want to live anymore, but after I got my job with Dr. Murphy, my friend Marcela took me to church, and I trusted Christ."

"You got religious?"

Her sister had been spouting her views of God, and she didn't know the first thing about Him. "No, I got forgiven. I went to church for a while, but then I started listening to you tell me how God couldn't ignore my sins, and I quit going. I stopped talking to Him and reading my Bible. I'm beginning to see I wasn't thinking." Holly tensed her shoulders. "Tell me how you can presume to know how God thinks when you don't open His Word."

Diana's shoulders slumped, and she stared at her hands. "I don't know. You remember how demanding Mom was with us -- always harping on our responsibilities around the house. Nothing we did satisfied her. I think of God the same way. If we could never please Mom, how can we please God? How can God overlook what you did?"

"I'm just learning these things. I know Mom never made us feel worthy, but God's different. If I confess what I did wrong, He'll forgive me. The same is true of you. You keep pointing a finger at all my failings, but none of us are perfect. Even you."

Diana pushed her salad around on her plate. "I don't like to talk about Mom. I don't want to talk about God, either."

"I know, but you and I are all that's left of Dad. He wouldn't want us to live in the past, trapped by our weaknesses. He'd encourage us to keep going. Maybe you don't care to hear about it now, but God can help you to overcome our childhood. I'd like to help you, but first we have to try to get along." A glint of hope softened Holly's nerves.

"I'll try." Diana nodded before she looked at her

watch.

Holly touched her sister's hand. "Why does what I did trouble you so much? I'd like to understand."

Diana's eyes filled with tears. She leaned back in her seat and ran her hand along the napkin in her lap. "Red and I -- can't have children." She shook her head, then bounded to her feet, grabbing the check. "Let me get this."

"I'm sorry, Diana."

She rushed toward the cashier clutching the bill.

Her sister's inability to slow down -- it all made sense now. She was running from her problems and would continue to go in circles until she ran into God.

Holly took a sip of iced tea and gazed at the traffic moving with starts and stops through the red light at the end of the block. Wow, she hadn't dreamed her sister carried such a heavy burden. She thought Red and Diana didn't have kids because Diana didn't want to mess up her figure. A wave of guilt careened through her. *Oh, my dear sister. I feel your pain, desiring with all my heart to be a mother.*

Time to go back to work. Holly looked around for her purse. The chair on the other side of the table scraped against the floor. She yanked her head up. A man dropped into the seat across from her where Diana had sat.

"Hi, Holly. Diana said I might find you here today. It's been a long time."

~

Holly lowered herself to her couch without leaning back. She tapped her knees then wrung her hands. The ability to concentrate on her patients this afternoon had challenged her. Zack's sudden appearance sent her reeling. He was the last person she'd expected to see.

What could he possibly want to talk about? He claimed he was sorry for the past and made her believe he needed a few moments to tell her how he felt. Was she too gullible?

Her excuse that she needed to get back to work had come in handy. But how had he convinced her to allow him to visit her apartment? *Lord, I couldn't -- I wouldn't go back to those days. Not anymore. I'm a Christian now.*

The doorbell chimed. Maybe she shouldn't answer it. She pulled herself up and smoothed her jeans. Why had she put on her most attractive top, the jade green that matched her eyes? She didn't have feelings for him anymore. Why try to impress him?

A well built, blond man, his hair in a spiky style, smiled at her when she opened the door. "Hi, Holly. I brought some wine." He held up the bottle of red Chardonnay.

She stepped back and allowed him to enter. "I'll get you a glass, but I don't want any. Thank you."

"You don't drink anymore?" He strolled in and glanced around at her hall and living room.

"Not really. I've lost the taste for it. Sit down." She motioned to the easy chair.

"Then let's not open it."

"All right." The bottle remained on the counter. She sank down on the couch across from him.

Zack squirmed in the chair before crossing his ankle over his knee. "It's been a long time, Holly. My life's different. I suppose I've matured." He uncrossed his legs and put his hands on his knees. "I'm sorry about how we left things. I was a stupid jerk for not staying in touch. How have you been doing?"

You were a guy who didn't want a crippled girlfriend. "Okay. A lot has changed for me, too." The clock over the fireplace ticked, counting each silent second that passed.

His gaze dropped to her jeans. "You don't seem to have much trouble with your prosthesis. You're doing a great job."

"It was hard at first, but I'm an expert at disguising it now."

"I've been thinking for a long time about what happened." He stood and sat on the couch next to her. "Everything was my fault. I have nightmares about the accident."

"Why are you telling me now?"

Zack's blue eyes swam behind tears.

Could the man be sincere?

"I was too much of an idiot at first. I didn't think about it. I put it out of my mind. Then I went to law school and got married."

"You're married?" Holly stiffened.

"No, Holly." He lowered his voice. "I wouldn't be here if I was, though I still would've found a way to talk to you. I'm divorced. My marriage didn't last long. My wife left and took our baby daughter a year ago."

He didn't know he had another son or daughter in heaven. "I'm sorry."

"Yeah, I didn't want the divorce. She did." He raked his hand through his hair.

Dare she even ask? "What happened?"

"I don't know. I blame myself, but I suppose I

became distant. I tell you honestly, I've never been able to get over what I did to you." Zack stood and paced her living room. "I feel the weight of guilt every day."

Her former boyfriend needed the Lord. "Why don't you ask God to forgive you?"

"God? What about you? I need to ask your forgiveness." He returned to the couch and held her hand.

What was he after? Surely he didn't want to reestablish their relationship. She wanted no part of that.

"I do forgive you." She pulled her hand away. "But at first I had to ask God's forgiveness.

"For what? You didn't do anything wrong." He furrowed his brow as his voice broke and a tear coursed down his clean-shaven cheek.

"There was something I didn't tell you." She pushed up and limped toward the kitchen, exhausted from disguising her disability all day. Just a glimpse of her Bible sitting on the table gave her strength. "When I got on the bike with you, I... I was..." She turned around.

He stood in front of her.

"Was what, Holly?" His words were only a whisper.

"Two people were on the back of your motorcycle with you that day."

"What do you mean?"

"I was pregnant."

"Pregnant? But where..." He grasped her hand. "Holly, where's our child?"

"The baby died that night, the same night I lost my leg."

"Why didn't you tell me?" He held both her hands, a tortured look on his face.

"Would it have made any difference?" Determined not to yield to a wave of pity, she pushed past him.

He pulled her to him. "I'm so sorry for what I put you through. I don't know if there's a chance, but I'd like to make it up to you. Start again."

"Why? To continue to appease your conscience? Look, Zack, I told you I don't hold you responsible any more. We were both stupid college kids. Neither of us knew any better though we should have. Let's just leave it at that." This man didn't need her. He needed God in his life.

"I'll be waiting for you if you change your mind." He turned toward the hall. She'd never seen him look so sad.

"I'm in love with someone else. The Lord first and a wonderful Christian guy." She'd just admitted her feelings out loud -- to a man she hadn't seen in years.

"There's no room in your life for me. I can see that." Zack nodded. "I understand, but thank you for not holding anything against me. I needed to hear it."

"I couldn't have made it without the Lord. You may want to seek His mercy and get to know Him." Zack had carried a burden Holly wasn't aware of. She thought he'd put her out of his mind after he'd abandoned her at the hospital.

"It's hard for me to believe you could excuse what I did. You must have a powerful God on your side."

Zack opened the apartment door and reeled back toward her on the threshold. A grateful look softened his gaze. He pulled her close and whispered in her ear. "Thank you for not hating me." He kissed her cheek, curved around to pace down the hall, and disappeared into the elevator.

She watched him go. As she turned, a movement at the other end of the hallway caught her attention.

Another man stood ten feet from her apartment door, his mouth open.

"Jess?"

"I see you're busy. Another time, Holly." He lumbered to the elevator.

~

Jess parked his car on the street and meandered the two blocks to Puget Sound Brewery, the hottest gathering place in the area. The sun set low on the horizon as he inhaled a breath of pleasant air. He ran a hand over his damp forehead. He couldn't refuse William Oatman's invitation to his Hawaiian send off. They'd think he resented the guy if he didn't show. Besides, he needed to get his mind off Holly. Was he nervous because he was going into a bar for the first time since he'd quit drinking, or because he'd seen Holly hugging some man in her apartment?

He'd taken the elevator down to her floor hoping she'd go for a walk with him. Then the guy stepped out, pulled her into an embrace, and kissed her cheek. To make matters worse, he was muscular and slim, everything Jess wasn't. She looked awful cozy with the Greek god in an Armani suit.

They lived in a free world. She had every right to date. Jess and Holly were only friends after all. They'd made that clear after their kiss. Still, he somehow had the idea she cared about him. Maybe he was wrong. She probably stopped looking on the inside and took a glimpse at the outside -- his fat body. He didn't blame her. It had all been too good to be true anyway. He was a fool to think he could attract a woman like Holly.

The glass door opened when he pulled the brass handle. The aroma of beer hit him the minute he walked in. No hiding the fact they produced their own brand onsite.

The desire for a drink overwhelmed him, something he hadn't experienced for a couple of years.

"Hey, Jess." William met him at the long mahogany bar. "Thanks for coming, buddy. We're back here in the Frazier room."

Intimate booths lined the dark paneled walls. A single bell shaped light hung above each table. He followed William to the small room off the main bar.

"Grab you a tall mug. It's on me."

A crowd of at least twenty gathered for the send-off party. Glasses of beer lined the top of a portable bar. A table was laden with crackers and a cheese ball, tiny sausages, sandwiches, and chips and dip.

Pat waved at him. "Hi, Jess. Things just aren't the same without you at the office." She nudged her husband Terry standing next to her. "He's the guy who gets to work at home now. I'm jealous of you, getting an extra hour of sleep since you don't have to make the commute."

Terry stuck out his hand. "Yeah, it's even worse for me. I have to drive north to Kingland every day. How ya doing, Jess?"

"Pretty good. I guess I'm spoiled." Jess shook the man's hand.

"Hey, come on, buddy. You look like you need a drink." Terry grabbed his arm and led him to the bar. "There you go." He pointed to a frosty mug.

The glass felt cool and moist in Jess's hand. The suds bubbled, inviting him to take a taste. He caught a whiff of beer on tap, the aroma like no other smell. With an unsteady hand, he lifted the glass to his lips.

His heart pounded. Did he really want to go back to his drunken ways, his lowered inhibitions, another act of disobedience toward the Lord? He took a deep breath and set the mug back down on the table. "On second thought, I think I'll grab a diet soft drink instead."

Jess exited the Frazier room and walked up to the bar.

The bartender met him by the cash register. "Yes, sir?"

"Give me a sugar-free soda, please." Jess pulled out a five. A familiar, obnoxious laugh caught his attention. He turned toward a table two spaces down from the bar. Just as he'd thought. Loud-mouthed George Colton leaned toward a dark haired woman who didn't look old enough to be in a bar. His hands roamed all over her.

Jess picked up the coke and moved closer to the booth. "Well, if it isn't my cousin up to his old tricks. Why don't you take your hands off the lady?"

George wrenched his neck around to look at Jess. "My loser cousin."

"Yeah? Well, at least I know how to treat a woman with respect." Even if George was drunk, he had no excuse for his behavior.

"You're just as uppity as your father. You pig. You couldn't even get a woman if you tried." He took a swig of beer.

His companion pushed free of him. "I wouldn't be so sure. I'd rather be seen with somebody like him than a drunk like you."

George scowled and downed his beer.

"Well, on that note, I'll get back to my friends." He turned around and made his way to the Frazier room. That's all he needed, to run into his lush of a cousin. Seeing George reinforced his decision to never slide back into the old life. How could he have allowed himself to entertain thoughts of drinking again? Even if he remained a fat slob forever, he couldn't go back to using alcohol.

Though he wanted to erase the memory of Holly with another guy, he couldn't do it with booze. One addiction was enough.

Chapter Nine

The next morning in front of his apartment building, Jess parked, turned off the ignition, and rubbed his cheeks, still warm from Dr. Van Zant's scolding. His doctor shattered any illusions Jess may have harbored. He was no longer pre-diabetic but suffered from full blown diabetes -- something he couldn't ignore any longer if he wanted to remain on this earth.

His computer waited upstairs, but he didn't want to return to the confines of his apartment yet. The gardens where Holly fell asleep on his shoulder, where he'd kissed her and called her Snow White, would be a good place to unwind and digest the twists and turns his life had taken.

The picture of the slim blond man with his arms around Holly continued to drift into his thoughts uninvited, offering him no peace. Now, after the doctor's report, discouragement dimmed his hopes of having a life with her. But he needed to get his disease under control.

The swing beckoned. He eased back, setting the chair in motion with his feet. The sun moved closer to the western horizon. Dusk would fall in another couple of hours.

The doctor's words blasted into his brain demanding attention. Lose a minimum of a hundred pounds, and more would be better. Dr. Van Zant laid out the facts -- get healthy or die at an early age. Overeating was no longer an option if Jess wanted to live to be an old man.

Did he even care? What did he have to live for? A withered blossom from a lilac bush dropped to the ground. Like him -- if he didn't take control of his life.

He gave himself a mental reprimand. God hadn't abandoned him.

The doctor had summed up Jess's first option. Begin taking medication and follow a diet for diabetic patients. The set of colorful brochures with suggested meal plans were tucked in an envelope still in his car. If he couldn't control his diabetes with medication, he'd have to go on insulin.

But reality lurked, and he couldn't deny it. He had issues to work on before he could manage his diet. His father would be the biggest hurdle. If he wanted to escape the maze of his addiction, he'd have to learn how to deal with his fear of displeasing Dad.

He grabbed a handful of hair and yanked. He couldn't blame it all on a faulty relationship. Self-control, one of the fruit of the Spirit, defied him. Moisture covered his forehead. There. He'd admitted it.

"Is this a private swing, or can anyone join you?" Holly's smile replaced his somber thoughts. A light brown tee shirt brought out the copper tones in her hair.

"Yes, ma'am. I was saving this spot just for you." He scooted over.

His chest tightened with another difficulty. Would she mention anything about her visitor? What should he say if she did?

Holly squeezed in next to him and clasped her hands under her chin. "I'm sorry you rushed off the other day. I was just saying good-bye to an old friend."

"From the way he hugged you, he must be a close, old friend." Jess flinched. Now he'd unveiled his jealousy and couldn't call the words back.

Her warm fingers glided over his hand. "He was someone from my past, the guy I told you about." She bit her lip. "That relationship died the day... the day he walked out on me."

"Looked like he might have changed his mind." The lump in Jess's stomach turned rock hard. "I'm sorry, Holly. This doesn't concern me."

She returned her gaze to his face. "I think it does." Her whispered message confused him.

He scrunched his nose. What else could he say? Her words brought a fragment of hope, but hope of what? A wife who lived with a fat, diabetic husband? He couldn't do that to her.

"I'm here for you as a friend," he said.

"I know, and because you are, Zack is part of my past and will remain there."

Jess's churning emotions prevented anymore conversation about the guy. "How was your day?"

"The dental clinic kept me busy as usual." She sighed. "I had a young blind patient who thought his condition gave him an excuse for his hands to investigate the space around my chair. Had to dodge him a couple of times." She chortled and gave the swing a push.

Jess scratched his head. "So if I was blind, I wouldn't have to watch my hands around you?"

"Oh, yes, you would." She gave him a playful poke.

"Don't worry. My mom taught me to be a gentleman." Jess liked the lighthearted banter.

"I can tell. You stood when Diana came up to our table the other day. Not too many men have manners these days, and she treated you horribly. I'm still fuming. You were so sweet to her, and she didn't deserve it."

"I've forgotten it." *Faded away with all the other reactions to my size.*

"You know a lot about forgiveness."

Forgiveness? Yeah, except where my father's concerned.

"How's your work going?" She smiled.

Maybe he shouldn't tell her about the doctor's report. It'd only worry her. But then he needed her prayers. "I had to take some time off today and see my doctor. Unfortunately the report was negative. Seems I'm diabetic. If I don't get my blood sugar down, he says I could go into a diabetic coma. I'm sure he's just trying to scare me."

"Wow, Jess. I'm sorry. Let me know how I can help. Maybe make you a fat-free meal or go jogging with you."

"Really?" Her non-judgmental words blessed him. A treasure he could hide deep within to garner when he needed encouragement.

"Yes. I don't want anything to happen to you." She leaned against him and blinked her green eyes.

"Thank you for not lecturing me." The swing must be a good place to kiss, because he desired with all his heart to take her in his arms. He scooted a bit to face her.

"Holly, I... I..."

She looked into his eyes and leaned closer.

Why was he hesitating? He slid his thumb down her velvety soft cheek, commanding his pounding heart to slow but to no avail. He gazed into her verdant green eyes and took what he longed for -- her lips. Shutting the rest of the world out, he savored her nearness and wrapped both arms around her. Her perfume's scent sent fire down his spine to his stomach. Finally, with reluctance, he moved away but knew he wouldn't be satisfied with only one kiss. *So this is what it's like to fall in love.*

Holly hadn't backed off. From the way she'd nuzzled into his embrace, he knew -- she enjoyed the kiss. Maybe the dude from her past wasn't a threat after all.

She touched her finger to her lips and gave him a look that set his heart pounding again. "Jess, please take care of yourself. I need for you to stay well."

Though Holly provided strong motivation to become healthy, his bad habits had harassed him for a long time. *Lord, I need You to help me do this.*

He gave a short whistle. "I'm asking for your prayers. I don't think it's going to be easy. You see, Holly, I suspect I'm dealing with an addictive--"

The vibration in Jess's pocket tickled before he heard the phone's chirp. "Excuse me." He checked the caller ID. "Hi Sis. What's going on?"

"Mom's been admitted to Bayview Hospital. They're not sure what's wrong. Can you come right away?"

A dizzy wave circled through his head. *Dear Lord, take care of her.* "Sure. I'm on my way." He stuffed the cell back in his pocket and ran a hand through his hair. "I need to go to the hospital. Come with me. We can pray for my mom on the way."

~

Holly had never seen Jess move so fast. The front entrance doors slid open. He reached the information booth before she did.

"Mrs. Colton's been taken from emergency to the fourth floor, room 433. You can see her now. Family members only, however." The gray-haired woman straightened a pile of papers and leafed through them. The phone rang, and she picked it up.

"Here's the closest elevator." Jess pointed to their right.

"Are you okay?" His face was fraught with concern.

Holly slipped her arms through his after the elevator door closed.

He grasped her hand, lifted it to his lips, and kissed her fingers. "Thank you for coming with me and praying on the way over. You'll never know what a support you are to me."

"Did Margaret say what they suspected?" She patted his hand and gave him a shy smile.

"No. I'd imagine now she's left emergency, they'll be calling her regular doctor."

"You don't suppose it's diabetes?" *The disease ran in families, didn't it?*

The elevator stopped with a jolt. "Well, I don't know, but I doubt it." The door slid open.

"Which way?" Holly said.

"Looks like 433 would be to the left." Holly

matched her strides to Jess's. She glimpsed at the hallway past the nurse's station. A series of pictures with metal plates underneath hung along the wall. Past and current hospital administrators.

"Room 429, 431, this is it. 433," Jess said.

Holly clutched his arm. "The information clerk said family only. I'd better stay out here."

Jess looked down at her. The pain in his eyes touched a tender place in her heart. He leaned toward her and drew her near, like a warm blanket wrapping around her. Could she feel him trembling? He shifted away and offered a half smile. "All right. I'll be back when I find out something."

Holly squeezed his hand. "You have my prayers." When she looked up, Margaret craned her neck out the door, a frown on her face, before following her brother back inside in the room.

Holly hated hospitals. They evoked a rush of memories better left in the past. The day of the accident she'd almost died at the scene. Neither she nor Zack had a cell phone and few cars passed them on the country road. When the ambulance finally arrived, shock and blood loss had almost defeated her. She'd wished for death in that moment.

The experience had brought her more of an understanding of the brevity of man's existence on earth -- one reason Jess had grown so important to her. He yearned for God the way she did.

The day Zack visited her apartment, she knew she loved Jess. Fear rippled up her spine. What would Jess say if he learned she'd been pregnant and careless enough to risk the life of her child?

Holly plopped down in one of the two chairs

outside the door.

She stared at her shoes as she leaned forward, her head in her hands. "Lord, please bring healing to Jess's mother. Then I ask you to heal Jess. This compulsion holding him, bring him freedom from it. Guard our relationship and allow it to bloom if it is Your will. In Jesus name."

"Holly?" The voice drew her from the prayer. Margaret stood over her, sending an angry glare down at her.

Holly jumped up from her chair and swayed on her prosthesis a moment. "Oh, Margaret. I was praying for your mother. How is everything?"

Jess's sister stood motionless then tossed a strand of straight brown hair off her cheek. "Mom collapsed at home with severe pain in her right side below the rib cage. She had nausea and couldn't stop vomiting. Dad called 9-1-1."

"I'm sorry."

"Dr. Stephen was here. She suffered a gallbladder attack. I think he's coming back in the morning after the test results are in to determine if she needs surgery."

"I'll pray she doesn't."

Hardness she hadn't noticed during dinner at the Colton's home lined Margaret's face.

"Do you really think prayer will do any good?" She waved her hand, pointing to the chair where Holly had sat.

"Yes, God says He wants us to pray."

Margaret shrugged. "To each his own. Look, I'm glad we have this time to talk. I noticed you and Jess are rather chummy." She cleared her throat. "The way he had his arms all over you."

An orderly pushed a patient in a wheelchair down the hallway toward the nurses' station. Holly lowered her voice. "I care a lot about your brother. He's a fine Christian man."

Margaret's gaze traveled down the length of Holly. "You're a very attractive woman. You could probably have any man you wanted."

"I'm not concerned about just any man." Holly shook her head. "Jess is a considerate, moral person, and he loves God."

A nurse carrying a clipboard strolled into the room next to Mrs. Colton.

Margaret folded her arms. "I've never understood his attraction to religion."

"He loves the Lord. Jess goes to church to worship God and--"

"You don't need to tell me about my brother. I'm well acquainted with him. I've known him for thirty-two years. What do you want anyway?"

Holly gasped. "I don't know what you mean?"

Margaret pointed a finger in her face. "My brother is a vulnerable, sensitive man. At his weight, I can't imagine any woman being interested in him. If you dare break his heart, I'll... I'll..."

"How can you think I'm after anything from Jess except his friendship?" Holly stepped toward Margaret, her palms raised. "Why are you so upset with me simply because I like spending time with your brother?"

Margaret's lips trembled. "Jess is fragile. I see how our dad's words cut him, and it hurts me. I won't let you wound him, too. I'll protect Jess from you if I have to." She whirled around and traipsed back into her mother's hospital room.

Holly's mouth gaped. The audacity of the woman.

Though Margaret's words stung, Holly needed to stuff her ill-feelings. Now she'd have to prove to this family she was worthy of Jess. But was she?

~

Jess gazed down at his mother's ashen face -- stark white against the hospital sheets. Though doting, his mom had always provided stability. To see her pale and helpless tore him apart. "Mom, I'm here." He touched her hand. "I love you."

Margaret had stepped outside, and Dad fixed his gaze out the window, giving Jess a private moment with her. She opened her eyes, blinked, and raised the corners of her mouth. "Son, I'm going to be fine. Now don't you worry about me."

He lowered himself to the chair beside her bed. "I know you are. Holly's outside, and we've been praying for you."

"Holly's a nice girl." His mom smiled again and closed her eyes. She needed her rest.

Jess rose and clasped a hand on his father's shoulder before turning toward the door. When Margaret pushed past him, she moved to Mom's side.

Holly sat slumped in a chair near the door.

"Hey, Holly."

Her large eyes appeared tired. He'd probably added a lot of stress to her day.

"Are you ready?"

She nodded, her usual smile absent.

"Holly?"

"I'm just worn-out."

"Let's get you home." He reached for her hand and helped her up as they trudged toward the elevators.

"How's your mom?"

"Weak, but I think she's going to be fine."

Holly's smile didn't return.

"The church is on our way. Would you mind if we stop in to pray for my family?"

She shook her head. "No. I'm never too exhausted to pray."

"I wouldn't ask you if I didn't think it important."

He parked in the side lot, now empty except for a few vehicles and the church bus. It was still early. The Wednesday night youth club wouldn't meet for another hour.

Jess grasped Holly's hand when they strolled in through the front door to the altar. She gripped his arm as if she needed support to kneel on the padded railing along the length of the stage. He bowed his head, never releasing his hold while they prayed. "Lord, thank you for my friend Holly who cares enough to pray with me. I lift up my family to You. Please bring healing to Mom, but I also ask You to bind us together as a family, freeing us from the things which keep us apart."

Jess offered his hand again when she rose with an unsteady movement. Tears streamed down her cheeks. He hadn't imagined she'd get this emotional over a prayer. Maybe she was worried about his mom. He wrapped her in another hug. "Thanks for being there for me."

She dabbed her eyes with a tissue. "I'm sorry."

He wiped a remaining tear from her cheek. "It's okay, Holly."

They headed down the aisle toward the foyer. He

stopped a moment and looked to the front. Would they ever take these steps as bride and groom? Though the possibility seemed out of reach now, God willing, it would happen one day.

"Hello, there." A young man emerged from the side door near the front and extended his hand when he got closer. "I'm Timothy Garrett, the new youth pastor."

"Oh, yes. Looks like you're just in time for the kids to start back to school. It's good to meet you." Jess nodded toward Holly. "This is Holly Harrison, and I'm Jess Colton. Welcome to Woodlyn Fellowship."

Timothy flashed a wide smile displaying white teeth. Gel-spiked strands of dark brown hair poked up on his head. "Nice to meet you two. Call me Tim."

"Great. Guess you're headed for the youth meeting."

His face lit up. "Yep, my first night with the kids. Pray for me. I'm going to need it."

"You bet. It's been a pleasure." Jess held out his hand again.

The youth pastor hadn't arrived any too soon. Woodlyn needed someone to guide them, especially since teen attendance had taken a downward spiral lately.

A pink sky silhouetted the dark blue mountains in the distance. Navy clouds scattered across the heavens. He pulled his attention to the sweet woman by his side. His heart told him he loved her.

Jess reached for Holly's hand and basked in the comfortable silence on the drive back to the apartment. She had assured him the old boyfriend would remain in her past. The doors to their relationship swung wide open, or did they?

What about his weight? He couldn't even walk

without puffing. The thought jarred him. The gate to his future with Holly squeaked and slammed shut, closing him out. He had the key in his hand, but until he controlled his gluttony, the door would remain locked.

Chapter Ten

With Holly's workday finally over, she updated her last patient's chart and filed it. She pulled her cell phone out of her pocket. No message from Jess yet.

The first day after his mom's admission to the hospital, his text came in early -- in plenty of time to pray about the doctor's decision to remove Mrs. Colton's gall bladder. Text messages were fine, but she preferred a phone call. Yesterday's conversation eased her concern. The doctor had released Jess's mother and things looked good.

She took the elevator to the parking garage. When she settled behind the wheel and drove out, Marcela followed in her old Chevy. Holly waved and turned onto the main road.

At the first red light, she braked and tapped her fingers on the dashboard. Margaret's words still bothered her. Getting them off her mind wasn't easy. How could Jess's sister think Holly meant him harm?

The light flashed green, and she curved onto the street toward her apartment complex. Diana and Jess's sister were alike in many ways. Overprotective and overbearing. Neither understood how Holly could love a big guy like Jess. She didn't see rolls of fat when she looked at him, just his gorgeous blue eyes, his handsome face, and the tender lips that kissed her. Most important she envisioned the Christian man inside. Heavy or not, he made her heart sing.

She admitted she wanted to be a wife and mother more than anything. Marriage to Jess -- she could dream all day about it. But he needed to know about her handicap before they pursued thoughts of getting married. Maybe he'd change his mind or have doubts like Zack did at first. She shuttered. Surely not.

Would there ever be a right time to tell him? Maybe soon. She had to give the guy a chance to back out of their relationship before things got too serious.

How would Jess react when she told him about the miscarriage? He said he didn't judge her for sleeping with Zack and that he'd be a hypocrite if he did. What had he meant? He must have done some things he wasn't proud of either.

Then she thought of Margaret's warnings. Perhaps she was right. Holly wasn't fit for a fine man like Jess, yet she reminded herself Jesus forgave her for the ugly mistakes in her life.

Her phone chirped as she pulled into the parking garage at Rainier Regency.

"Hello, Miss Holly. Just checking to see if you'd gotten home yet." Her breath caught at Jess's calming voice.

"Yes, I'm parking now. Should be up in five minutes."

"I'm thinking about running over to the Woodlyn Farmers' Market to pick up some fresh veggies and look at the booths. Seven straight hours of concentration has fried my brain. Wanta go?"

Holly climbed out of her car and clicked the locks. "Sure. I can meet you in the lobby. I need to check my mail anyway."

"When I see you don't mention anything about query screens." His soft chuckle soothed her.

She couldn't help but laugh. "I can promise you even if I knew what one was, I wouldn't say a thing. Thanks for the report on your mom. Sounds like she's going to be fine." She stepped into the elevator and punched *Lobby*.

"I went to see her early this morning. She looks good." He wheezed. "How are you today? You seemed like something might've been bothering you when we came home from the hospital."

She'd hoped he hadn't noticed her tension after Margaret's reprimand, but obviously he had. His ability to observe her emotions surprised her. A lot of guys were oblivious to women's feelings. "I'm rested now. No need to worry about me." The elevator stopped at the lobby. "See you shortly."

She hated to tell a fib, but Jess couldn't know what his sister had said. He already suffered a rift with his father. Holly couldn't open the door for more problems between Jess and a family member though the weight of Margaret's words still bore on her.

~

Jess parked on the far side of the Farmers Market Pavilion and glanced at Holly next to him. She got prettier every time he saw her. He exhaled a contented sigh. Maybe he had control of his life after all. He grasped her hand as they strolled toward the building.

Jim had been pleased with the forward movement of Jess's work when he'd turned in his weekly report last Friday. Guess he'd have to keep up the eleven hours a day work schedule for now though the additional time put a strain on his weight-loss efforts.

He needed to force himself to get down to the apartment gym and reduce his food intake. He chuckled under his breath. *Maybe I should visit Diana's gym.* Of course, knowing what you need to do and doing it were two different things.

A large opening led into the market. Jess breathed in the clean air filled with the aroma of cut flowers, fresh bread, and fish. He put his arm around Holly's shoulder and gave it a squeeze. "My uncle owns a farm in the area, but none of these booths say Colton's." What a relief to walk through the crowded market place with Holly by his side -- to get his mind on something besides diabetes, gall bladders and defining data processing needs. "The fruit and veggies taste a lot better than what you can buy in the grocery store. I can't decide what to get."

Holly grinned. "Don't try to make another stir-fry with them." She made a slow turn in the middle aisle. "I can't decide which booth to look at first. This one sells lavender products. Hmm. Room spray, potpourri bags, or lavender tea?" She fingered a blue and purple cloth bag of lavender tied up with a piece of lace.

He loved seeing her happy and relaxed. The day in the swing after she'd fallen asleep, he understood her stress. Sometimes she mystified him, though. He picked up a vibe on occasion. There was a part of her life she kept private. Certain moods didn't make sense, like the time she got upset about him wanting to wade at the beach in Eliot Bay -- a clue she held something back.

"Look at the herbs in these terra cotta flower pots." She bent over a vendor's table. "Dill, basil, saffron, thyme."

"I think I'll buy some of these juicy peaches and plums." Jess pointed to a farmer who held up half of a purple plum. "Want to try one?"

Holly lifted the fruit to her lips. "It's delicious."

After placing his selection on the scales, he gave the farmer a twenty. The guy counted out his change before sliding the peaches and plums into a bag.

The next booth displayed colorful bouquets of dalais, tiger lilies, sunflowers, baby's breath, and verbenas. The flowers rested in a vial of water and were wrapped in a piece of purple foil. He pointed to an arrangement. "I'll take one, please."

After he paid for the flowers, he passed the bouquet to Holly. "For a pretty lady, attractive even when she's covered in mud." A kiss on her cheek brought a warm glow to her face.

"Thank you. I love them." She cradled the bouquet in her arms.

He gathered up squash, organic lettuce, tomatoes, and cucumbers at the next booth. "Guess this is about all I came to buy. Need anything else?"

"No, I think these flowers are all I want." Holly sniffed the blossoms.

At the end of the pavilion by the door to the parking lot, a vendor juggled peaches in front of a booth. Jess whispered. "I don't want to think of the messy pile of fruit I'd have if I tried that."

He slid his arm around her slim waist. When they

got closer to his BMW, he unlocked the doors with his remote key.

"Well, if it's not my old cousin, Jess. And look here. I was wrong. You can get a beautiful woman to hang out with you."

Jess twisted to his left. Cousin George, his thorn in the side.

The strong odor of alcohol emanated from him. "How ya doing, cuz."

"We better leave." Jess placed his hand on Holly's back heading toward the passenger side of his car. The sack with his purchases hung on his other arm. "He's drunk. This won't be good."

"How's my well-educated, well-*fed* cousin today?" A hiccup escaped George's throat.

"Uh, look. This isn't the time to play Family Feud. We were just leaving."

"Aren't you going to introduce me to the gorgeous woman you're with?" He poked Jess's shoulder.

Jess spoke in a low tone near Holly's ear. "Sorry about this." Grasping her arm, he walked her around the back of his car before turning to his cousin. He raised his open hand. "Tell you what. I'll catch up with you another time."

George stumbled closer to them. "How did a hefty guy like you get such a good-looking girlfriend?" His cousin reached out toward Holly and touched her arm. "George Colton, beautiful. What's your last name?"

She stepped behind Jess, a tight grip on his arm.

"George, you need to back off now. Come on, Holly." Jess opened the passenger door.

"Oh, I just want to get to know your friend. What do you do for a living, honey?"

"It's none of your concern." Jess growled.

"Oh, I see you work at The Happy Smile Center, Holly Harrison." George gave a disgusting laugh.

Holly gasped and clamped a hand over her name tag.

"Tell me." George raised the side of his lip. "Are you after Jess for his money?"

Jess's patience thinned as anger filled his gut. "I said *back* off, George. You're making a fool out of yourself."

"You gonna make me, *fat* guy." George sneered.

Jess raised his fists and moved closer to the obnoxious man.

His cousin thrust a hand on Jess's shoulder, giving him a hard shove. "This is for me and my father."

Jess stumbled backwards a few steps, slipped, and landed hard on his backside. His fruit and vegetables scattered over the pavement. If he could become invisible, he'd be happy.

George reached toward Holly again. "Come here, beautiful."

A grounded walrus couldn't be more stuck. Jess had to get to his feet and put a stop to this, despite his humiliation and awkward position. If he could get to his knees, he could push up.

Holly flung George's grip off her arm. "You stupid drunk. Take a hike." She reached down and extended her hand to Jess, holding the flowers with the other.

George shrugged. "Okay, little miss. Have it your way." He stumbled off in the direction of the market but looked over his shoulder. "See you around, cuz."

Jess staggered to his feet and gulped down a curse word. Shame crushed him. George had stooped to a new low this time. "I'm sorry. I can't believe he was so drunk." But worse than that, Jess hadn't been able to defend Holly.

~

Jess slumped down to the couch. He disliked his drunken cousin, but the truth crushed him. George Colton wasn't his enemy but the unwanted flesh that held him captive -- a foe worse than any human being. The memory of this afternoon became more than he could bear. He didn't even have the ability to protect Holly. A real man wouldn't have that problem.

The familiar tug gripped him like a noose around his neck and pulled him against his will toward the kitchen. The freezer contained a gallon of chocolate chip ice cream -- a formidable enemy. His hands shook as he scooped out a large mound and plopped it into a mixing bowl along with nuts and whipping cream. A voice somewhere within protested, yet Jess didn't listen.

He sat at the kitchen table. The chair groaned and his hips hung off the sides. With monstrous bites, he polished off the creamy, chocolaty contents of the dish and dug out the rest from the container, dropping the scoops into his bowl with more nuts and this time marshmallow sauce.

He paused in pain. The cold ice cream gave him brain freeze. The voice sounded again. *What are you doing? Why do you need this?*

Anxiety turned to self-loathing. Breathing hard, he swiped at something gooey running down his chin. He picked up the plastic bowl with the rest of the now partially thawed ice cream and hurled it toward the kitchen wall. The chocolate mixture splattered on the ceiling, the wall, and the floor. Nuts and chocolate chips slid down as if in competition to see which could get to the floor first.

Jess groaned. He put his hands over his eyes and laid his head on the kitchen table. His shoulders shook as he sobbed.

Chapter Eleven

Holly gathered her purse and water bottle. "Bye, Dr. Murphy. See you tomorrow." She waved as she left the dental office. Images of Jess sitting on the ground at the farmers' market clutched at her heart and angered her. His cousin had disgraced him.

She clicked open the locks on her Honda when she reached the parking lot on the bottom floor of the medical complex. Jess warned her about some of his disgruntled family members, but she'd never expected to meet anyone like George. Surely he behaved better when he wasn't drunk.

Sunbeams reflected sparkles of light off the shrubbery. The city of Woodlyn offered earthen baskets of summer flowers hanging from metal poles near the sidewalk. Holly tried to relish the few weeks they had left of September -- the balmy weather before the rains.

Since afternoon traffic had picked up, pulling onto the road from the parking garage took a few more minutes than usual. More time to think about Jess.

She'd fallen in love with him, but how did he feel about her? He probably cared about her as well, but love? In any case, the time had come for her to tell him about her disability -- if nothing else, to give him an opportunity to back out. She'd try to talk to him this afternoon.

Her lane of traffic slowed to a crawl as cars ahead blared their horns. Over her left rearview mirror, she saw what blocked the lane -- a city bus disabled by the side of the road. She fingered the button to switch the radio on, but decided to call Jess instead.

After four rings, she reached his voice mail. *That's odd. He always has his phone in his pocket or at least close to his computer. Maybe he's deep in thought.* "Jess. Give me a call when you get this message. I wanted to say hi."

The lane came to a virtual standstill. She might as well be patient. Resting her head on the back of her seat didn't help her relax.

Jess's report from his doctor disturbed her. Diabetes was nothing to mess around with. Could he go into a diabetic coma if his blood sugar remained high?

Why did he overeat? There were a lot of pluses in his life. He was a Christian, had a good job, a nice apartment, and he had her. Well, she supposed that could be considered a plus.

She scratched her head. Hunger couldn't cause Jess's excessive weight gain. He never overate around her. All the books she'd read on food addiction made her suspect Jess used eating as a means of relieving stress.

The line of traffic started moving after a wrecker hauled the disabled bus out of the way. She drummed her fingers on the wheel. Why hadn't he called her back yet?

At the apartment building, his car was parked in the usual spot in the garage. She took the elevator to the seventh floor. No use wasting time going to her own apartment. She couldn't wait any longer to see if he was okay.

Her heart pounded as she punched his doorbell. She tapped a nervous rhythm with her right foot. No answer. She rang the bell again then knocked. "Jess, it's Holly. Are you there?"

Nothing. Her breath came faster. He could be laying on the floor in a diabetic coma. Only one thing to do. Rush down to the apartment manager's office to get him to open the door.

Wait. What was wrong with her? Before she panicked, it'd be a good idea to check the lobby, and the pool, and the gardens -- every inch of the building, the library, the long couches near the glass windows.

She hurried through the outside door leading to the pool and stepped out into the fresh air. In the first pool designed for families, two women splashed around with some kids. She followed the path to the adult pool, passing the poplar trees and hydrangea bushes.

Jess wasn't there. She tapped her forehead. His car was in the parking lot. He wasn't answering his cell or door, and he wasn't anywhere she looked. Fear nagged at her insides. She needed to find him.

Only two more places to check. Could he possibly be in the gym? She rushed down the hall off the lobby to the small room with weight lifting equipment, a treadmill, an elliptical machine, and a bicycle. She stuck her head in. Someone left the TV blaring in the empty room.

Their vacant swing in the garden swayed with a gust of breeze. Maybe someone picked him up for a meeting. No, unlikely. He worked long, hard hours and to her knowledge hardly ever left the building.

The decision became clear. She'd go to the manager and get him to open up Jess's apartment. He could be laying unconscious on the floor.

Her legs didn't transport her fast enough into the building. Craig Schackelford's office was to the left. She pounded on his door.

"Yes, come in."

The door opened with a shove. Craig pushed his glasses back on his nose. A two-day growth of whiskers covered his cheeks and upper lip.

"Yes, ma'am." He tapped a set of papers on the desk and placed them in a folder.

"Mr. Schackelford, I'm Holly Harrison in 516. I got stuck in the elevator with Jess Colton about three months ago."

"Oh, yes. The elevator company has assured me the malfunction shouldn't happen again. How did you enjoy your meal? Your dinner companion gave me the receipt."

"It was great. Thank you." Holly bit the nail on her little finger. "I'm here because Jess isn't answering his door up in 728." Her hands shook. "I was wondering if you could open it with a pass key. I'm worried about him."

"We don't make it a practice to open up people's apartments. I'm sure he's just gone out for something."

She wrung her hands. "You don't understand. He works at home, and his car is in his parking space."

"Well, he could be at the pool or in the lobby. Maybe he went for a walk." The apartment manager glanced down at the folder he laid on his desk.

"Sir, I've checked everywhere in the apartment

complex. Look. I know you probably think I'm over reacting, but he's diabetic. I'm afraid he's unconscious."

Mr. Schackelford rubbed the stubble on his chin. "All right. Let's look into this." He unlocked a wooden cabinet hanging on the wall. Long rows of keys dangled from holders, each one with a tag listing the apartment number. Craig ran his thumb left to right then lifted a key. "Here we go."

Holly followed him to the lobby elevators past the potted plants. She couldn't restrain her tears when the doors opened at the seventh floor. Her lips trembled with a prayer as they approached Jess's apartment.

He raised his fist and banged on the door. "Hello. Anyone at home?" No answer. "Okay, we're going in."

~

Jess backed away from the set of lines and numbers on his computer screen, his eyes crossing. He couldn't think. The incident at the farmers' market bothered him more than he wanted to admit. It had taken an hour to clean ice cream off his wall. Yet he'd struggled against the temptation of buying another carton when he'd made a trip to the grocery store.

No doubt now. He battled a food addition. Food. A shelter from life's storms.

He was caught in a vicious circle. The more problems he had, the more he ate. The more he ate, the more difficulties he encountered. *Lord, how am I going to get off this merry-go-round?*

Since Holly had come into his life, the issues only compounded. He was in love with her. In fact, he wanted a permanent relationship, yet he couldn't ask her to commit to an obese, sick man. He couldn't strap her to an unhappy marriage where the groom threw ice cream at walls and was too heavy to make love to his bride. The more he thought about his relationship with her, the more he began to realize what he had to do.

Before they made commitments to each other, before he told her he loved her, he needed to call it all off. It broke his heart, but he had nothing to offer her.

The best thing to ever come into his life, and he was preparing to throw it all away.

His project waited. Jim and the corporate office at Evergreen Technologies had applied more pressure. With an involuntary swallow, he barely resisted the urge to eat the other half of the chocolate cake in his freezer.

Doubts rose in his mind. Maybe he'd have to give up this position, take a normal, everyday job, one not laden with stress around every corner. All his work and training gone to waste.

Jess wiped the cold moisture from his brow. An iron vise squeezed with a cruel grip. *Lord, I need You. Why are you so distant?*

At times, concentration came easier if he listened to music while he worked. When he was in high school, his mother used to complain because he did his homework with his cassette player blaring, but it helped him think.

He pulled his cell phone out, selected Christian rock from the playlist, and turned the volume up louder than usual. There. He brought his mind back to the problems he'd tried to troubleshoot for Vauxhall.

The clock on his office wall showed he'd been concentrating for over two hours. The music had helped. Now for a quick break. He pulled the earphones out. Loud voices rang in the hall. His jaw dropped when the lock turned, and the door swung open.

Craig Shackleford and Holly dashed into his entry.

"Jess!" She screamed. "Why didn't you answer your door?"

Mr. Schackelford rushed toward him. "Are you all right, sir? We knocked. I'm so sorry for barging in on you, but your friend suspected something might be wrong." The man pushed his glasses back and raked a hand through his hair. "Looks like you're okay. I apologize."

Jess stared at Holly. "I'm fine. I had music turned up loud."

"Why didn't you answer your phone? Even if you had your earphones on, your cell would've vibrated." Holly swiped at a tear on her face. "You scared me."

Jess glanced at his desk with his cell lying near the computer, earphones still attached. "Uh-oh. I turned it on silent with the vibrations off this morning before I read my Bible."

"Well, sir, if you're okay, I'll leave now. Your friend suspected a medical emergency. That's the only reason I intruded on your privacy." The manager backed out of the door, shutting it after him.

"I'm sorry, Jess, but I've been worried to death. When I couldn't get you on the phone, I thought something was wrong. I even noticed your car in the parking garage so I knew you hadn't gone anywhere."

Jess's heart clinched at the fear in Holly's eyes. He couldn't subject her to a life of panic. If he was going to break her heart, he should get it over with. For the good of both of them. "Holly, we need to talk."

Chapter Twelve

Jess held an open palm to the brown leather couch. "Please. Sit down."

Holly gave a wary glance around the room and lowered to the edge of the sofa. "I'm so sorry I entered your apartment like this. It's just... It's just I..." Another tear escaped. "Please forgive me. I thought something was wrong with you. I pictured you unconscious on the floor." She covered her face.

The sight of Holly in tears tore through him like a tornado mowing down a row of trees. He scooted next to her, drawing her toward him. "Shh, Holly. It's okay. I'm not mad or anything." Somehow, he had to forge ahead. He pulled away and reached in his back pocket for his handkerchief. "Take this."

She dabbed her eyes and lifted a troubled gaze to him. "I want to talk to you, too. I need to tell you how much I care about you, and something about... my past. It could change everything. You may not want to ever see me again."

Jess cringed. *Dear Lord. She's going to think I'm breaking off our relationship because of whatever she tells me.*

"Before you go on, I need to let you know

something about me." He maneuvered his bulk to face her. "This *will* change everything, I'm afraid." He raked a hand through his hair. "I care about you."

"I know we haven't talked about it, but I've fallen in love with you."

"Holly, don't. There's no future for us. That's what I wanted to tell you."

Her eyes widened. "But why, Jess?" She dabbed her face again with his handkerchief. "I don't understand. Maybe it's because you don't feel the same way."

"I want to tell you I'm in love with you, too, but I can't. It's best we don't see each other anymore."

A furrow creased her brow. "I don't know what my future would be like if I thought you weren't a part of it. Whatever it is, please, let's just work it out. I love you."

Until now, he hadn't been sure of her feelings, though he suspected it. Her words piled more pain on his aching heart. Though he knew he shouldn't, he pulled her into his embrace again.

She slid her arms around his shoulders, and her tears soaked his shirt. How could he do this to her? She had to know the truth. "You'd be miserable with me. I'm not all you think I am. I have an addiction, to food and before, I drank too much."

"I've never seen you drink." She patted another tear.

"I know. Ridding myself of one addiction made room for the other."

"There are groups. You can get help. I can help you. Jess, it's not the end of the world." Her eyes brightened.

He longed to whisk away the tears on her cheek and touch her lips with his, but he didn't. "That's not all. My health isn't good. I couldn't ask you to give yourself to someone who may die at an early age. As much as I want and desire you in my life, it can't be. My family's dysfunctional. My life is a mess. Why would you want to settle for me?" If she gave him a reason to believe they could make it work, he might fold, give into his desires.

"What about the 'for better or worse' promise people make to each other?" She pinned him with another look, expectation in her eyes.

"We're not married. I can't change, Holly. This addiction has encroached on me, and I don't see any way out. It's best you be rid of me before we make any commitments." His throat tightened.

Her voice softened as she gazed at him. "Do I need to remind you, with God all things are possible?"

His brittle tone sounded foreign to him. "Don't you think I've pleaded with Him hundreds of times? He hasn't answered my prayers. It feels like God is so distant. That isn't likely to change with my continued disobedience."

His mouth fell open at his own words. The truth had come out. He was too entrenched in his addiction to change, even when it meant losing the woman he loved.

She shook her head. "Don't say that."

"I can't ask you to strap yourself to a fat slob. If we were to marry, I cringe at the thought of what you'd say when you saw my body. It's not a pretty sight. It's obese and misshapen."

"Jess." She gazed at him with mournful eyes.

"You're so beautiful. Your shape is so lovely." Jess lowered his forehead into his hands.

Holly took a breath and blew it out in a steady stream. "You don't know what you're talking about. You honestly think you're the only one whose body isn't perfect."

~

Holly reached down and untied the string on her left tennis shoe. Could she really do this?

"What are you doing?" His questioning look accelerated the nervous pangs in her stomach.

She lifted a restraining hand and continued her work. With an unsteady grip, she pulled her sock off exposing the curved metal of her prosthesis limb.

Jess's eyes became the size of large plates. "Oh, good Lord, Holly. What happened?"

Folding her jeans to her knee, she exposed the entire device. After releasing the suction holding the hollow plastic casing over her knee stump, she set the entire leg next to the couch.

Her heart thundered when she dared a glance at Jess.

He sat motionless, his eyes wide open. "Why didn't you tell me?"

"Because I thought you'd cast me out of your life if you knew. Now do you see? You're not the only one with a flawed body." She leaned back against the couch, her stub barely meeting the end of the seat.

Her icy palms made her shiver when she wrapped her arms around herself. No turning back. She'd taken the risk and revealed her secret. He'd always know now.

"You haven't told many people," he whispered.

"No. Only my family, of course, and Dr. Murphy. Zack, too. The accident happened when I rode on the back of his motorcycle."

"I don't know what to say." He gazed at her with

woeful blue eyes.

She wiped away another tear. "After I came to know you, I figured you'd love me in spite of it. That's the kind of man you are. I didn't know how to tell you until now."

Jess eased off the couch and slowly knelt in front of her. He folded her jeans a little higher, gazed at her with eyes of love and compassion, then bent down.

She gasped.

He lowered his lips to the stub and kissed it, then gazed up at her again.

"I can't believe you did that. I love you for it."

Jess blinked, a grimace painted on his face. With a groan, he strained to sit back on the couch. He slid his arms around her. "You're right. It would've made no difference in how I feel about you, but this makes things even more difficult."

~

Holly's disclosure flabbergasted Jess. She disguised her handicap so well. He never had any idea, and he could tell it embarrassed her to show him. She put him first without considering her own discomfort.

Condemnation and doom immersed Jess like a man sentenced to die. Nothing would change. He had to make this sacrifice for her. "After today, I can't see you any more, Holly."

She said nothing, only cried.

His heart broke knowing he'd hurt her. But she'd thank him someday.

The sound of her sobs grew more intense.

"Holly, please." He wrapped her in another

embrace. The soft skin on her cheek felt warm. Her femininity overcame him, surrounded him like a cloud. How could he go on without her?

He stood and picked up her prosthesis, handing it to her. "You need to go. Forgive me, Holly. This is the hardest thing I've ever done." Tears threatened to choke him, but he had to remain strong, if only for her.

"Do you mean it?" She blinked. "Do you really want me to leave?" She looked up at him through wet lashes.

He swiped at his cheek. "Yes. I need you to leave." If she didn't go soon, he'd cry along with her -- or change his mind.

Her green eyes remained on him a moment longer, as if she didn't believe his words. Then she nodded. "Okay, Jess."

When she reattached her leg and stood, he moved to her side. "I wish things were different. I'm sorry for what I've put you through. Please forgive me." He wanted to hold her and never let her go.

Holly floated toward the entrance, without a hint of a limp.

The door closing sounded like a death knell. A groan rose from his throat, and he dropped to his knees. His life shattered into a thousand pieces.

~

Jess checked his freezer. Nothing to eat -- just a turtle ice cream pie he'd picked up at 31 Flavors. With a shaking hand, he drew it out, picked up a spoon, and sat down at the table.

The memories of her severed leg injected painful

darts into his heart. She'd kept her secret because she thought it would repulse him. He'd kissed her leg hoping she'd understand it didn't. Now she was gone forever.

His heart warmed to know she trusted him enough to reveal her prosthesis. But now he felt even worse. She'd taken a big step, and he flung her out of his life.

Never had he felt so conflicted. Memories of the past hour consumed him. He thrust a spoon into the pie, not bothering to cut off a piece. The chocolate, vanilla, and coffee ice cream with its chocolate fudge and nut topping would calm him and make the misery go away. Before he got up from the table, he finished the dessert.

When he finally stood, he threw the spoon in the sink in disgust. If he quickly tossed the empty foil plate in the garbage, would that change the truth -- that he'd eaten a whole pie in one sitting?

What kind of progress was that? Dr. Van Zant would've berated him had he known. The familiar guilt consumed him.

Vegetables and fruit. Only one thing to do. Go to the store. He picked up his handkerchief still lying on the couch. The damp cloth saddened him with thoughts of Holly's tears. Like a zombie, he left the apartment. What would he do if he saw her in the complex somewhere?

He had to get to his car. Recollections of all the times she'd glided along by his side taunted him. He'd never suspected the truth. Thoughts of her stump sent a wave of shock over him again. She'd endured so much and had been so brave.

Finally Anderson's Grocery. Could he appease the guilt with ingredients for another stir fry? He ignored the sluggish feeling overwhelming him but couldn't disregard the memories. Holly's laugh, her striking green eyes, the way he felt when he kissed her. If he didn't pull himself together, he couldn't go in the store.

An available shopping cart sat near the front door. He pushed down the aisle toward produce. A cold sweat broke out over his face and neck -- his breathing became shallow. A wave of nausea traveled from his stomach to his throat. He reached for the edge of the stand holding the individual apples and looked for a place where he could sit. Nothing. The room whirled. He clutched the shelf, grappling for support and sank to the floor. Apples tumbled to the ground on top of him. He stared at the fluorescent lighting. "Holly," he moaned as blackness beckoned.

Chapter Thirteen

Holly's stomach said it was time for dinner yet she couldn't tolerate food now. It only reminded her of Jess's enemy—the excess love of food.

For the second time this evening, she took off her prosthesis then swung her legs up onto the couch, and rested her head on the end pillow. Energy and motivation deserted her. She had to find her way back to her life before Jess.

Thoughts of his lips on her leg where the sharp, metal post had sliced through still stirred her. She'd found a kind, warm man only to lose him because he lacked the willpower to overcome his addiction, though she couldn't judge him. She had her own share of failings.

Maybe Diana was right. God didn't think she was good enough for happiness, a husband, and a family.

She covered her face but that didn't erase the memory of the last several hours. Sobs shook her shoulders. *God, do you still love me?* The verse she'd read this morning rushed into her heart. She hopped to the kitchen table, holding on to the furniture. The Bible still lay open to First John, Chapter One. "If we confess our sins, He is faithful and just and will forgive us our sins and purify us from all unrighteousness."

She held to the chair and sank to her knees on the kitchen floor. *Lord, when I first asked Your Son into my life, I confessed I was a sinner, but I never felt cleansed. I take You at Your word. You have forgiven my sins and purified me. Therefore, I can forgive myself. Now please, God, help Jess know how much You love him. Bring him freedom from the sin controlling him. Amen.*

Holly placed her hands on the chair's seat and pushed up with her right leg. She hopped back to the couch. Peace surged through her spirit. Peace given to her by God alone. She had a long way to go, but God's assurance washed over her for the first time since she'd become a Christian. *Father, I just lost the man I love. Yet, You bring me joy and confidence.* She closed her eyes and worshiped the Lord.

Her situation certainly hadn't provided peace. She'd have to live without Jess Colton, but despite the negatives, God blessed her. Maybe that's how He worked. Blessing in the midst of adversity. Seeing her through the fires of her life.

Whether Jess was in them or not, her days would go on. More than anything right now, she wanted him to be free. A spark, a tiny glimmer of hope, glowed within her. Maybe someday Jess would have control over his life.

~

"Thanks for joining me for lunch, Marcela." Holly took a bite of her turkey sub as she watched the traffic outside the window of Michael's Deli. "Guess I just needed to talk."

"I'm sorry to hear Jess broke up with you, *Chica*. Did you have strong feelings for him?" Marcela brushed a stand of her long brown hair off her round face.

"I could lie to you and say no, but I did." Holly raised an eyebrow. "I've got to get past it, though."

Marcela dabbed her mouth with her napkin. "Are you in love with him?"

"It's funny. The world would tell me I couldn't be in love with an obese man, but I am." Holly shook her head and took a sip of ginger peach tea. "Surely God didn't let me become attracted to him without a reason. I don't want to believe this is the end of our relationship."

Marcela patted Holly's hand. "You're in my prayers now just like the first time you went to church with me, *hija.*"

"You're a dear friend." Those days when Marcela nudged her toward the Lord glistened in her memory like precious jewels. She smiled as she rubbed a tear away. "My heart is breaking over him. Yet I feel so confident God's got things under control." She scratched her head. "But his car wasn't in his parking place this morning when I left. That's unusual for him because he works at home."

"Maybe he had a meeting."

"Could be." Yet she'd only known him to go to a meeting once since they'd become friends. Holly wouldn't allow her imagination to get away from her again. Jess had another meeting in Seattle, of course.

~

"Got a minute?" Marcela crooked her finger as she leaned into Holly's cubicle.

"Sure. Come on in here." She tossed the paper bib into the garbage can.

"The next guy on your schedule made his appointment a couple of days ago. He hasn't seen Dr. Murphy yet, but he insisted on having you clean his teeth, said he needed the cleaning before the exam. He's lucky you had a cancellation."

"Hmm. What's his name?" Holly straightened her mouth mirror, the probes, the scaler, and syringe on the metal plate.

Marcela glanced at her clipboard. "I believe it's... let's see... Colton. Hmm, same last name as Jess. George Colton."

Holly's mouth fell open. "Oh, no."

Marcela scrunched her nose. "What's the matter? Do you know him?"

"Sort of. He's Jess's cousin. An insufferable idiot -- the cousin, not Jess."

Marcela rolled her eyes. "I'm sorry you have to put up with him. Call if you need anything." She headed toward the main office.

Why would George Colton want her to clean his teeth? *If he gives me one ounce of trouble, he's out of here.* Dr. Murphy wouldn't stand for any impropriety.

Holly finished cleaning her instruments and straightened her table. She pushed the x-ray machine over to the side and picked up the chart Marcela left. With a reluctant sigh, she marched to the waiting room door. "Mr. Colton."

Jess's cousin laid his magazine down and grinned at her as he rose.

"This way please." She usually smiled at patients, but the memory of George pushing Jess to the ground still infuriated her. Would she really be able to clean his teeth? She might be tempted to poke him with an instrument. Maybe she should refuse to treat him.

He followed her to the cubicle, and she pointed to the chair. "You can sit there." His chart contained very little information. Either he had never seen a dentist before, or he didn't want to fill out the forms. She fastened the paper bib around him.

George settled back in the reclining chair, giving her a sheepish grin. "To be honest, I made this appointment because I wanted to talk to you."

She gasped and crossed her arms over her chest. The nerve of the guy -- using her workplace to flirt or whatever he came to do. "There's nothing to talk about."

He folded his hands in his lap. "I wanted to apologize for the my behavior at the market. Drinking too much is not a very good excuse. I usually don't act like that and hate the thought of you believing I'm a jerk." He tilted his head as if waiting for her reaction.

Holly's blood pressure rose. "It doesn't matter if *I* think you're a jerk. You need to save your apology for Jess."

"He doesn't want anything to do with me. I'm not intellectual enough." He ran a hand through his hair. "My cousin is nothing but a snob."

Snob would be the last word she'd use to describe Jess. How could George say that?

"But since I'm here, let me make it up to you. I'd like to take you to the Space Needle in Seattle." He ran a finger down her arm.

"Look." Holly jerked her hand away. "You're here under false pretenses. If you don't leave, I'm going to call Dr. Murphy."

He winked. "You're a beautiful woman. My cousin isn't your type anyway. You need a strong, virile guy." He reached for her waist.

"Like you, I suppose." The brash man didn't behave any better sober.

"Just let me take you to dinner. You're a hot chick, but I promise to behave."

When she yanked the bib from his neck, the metal chain slapped him in the chin as the clasp released. "Your cousin is one of the finest men I've ever met. I admire his character and his values. I'm sure he'd love to see the rift in your family mended if you'd give him a chance. But even if you were twice the man he is, I still wouldn't go out with you." She stormed out of the cubicle. "Dr. Murphy, I need your assistance, please."

~

Holly still fumed as she parked her car in her regular space at Rainier Regency. She could always count on Dr. Murphy to support her, like when he invited George to leave and suggested they'd charge his credit card if he ever pulled that stunt again.

Jess's car was still gone. He couldn't have moved away or left town this soon. A sick feeling inched into the pit of her stomach.

Instead of going to her apartment, she took the elevator to the seventh floor. She didn't want a repeat of yesterday when Mr. Schackelford opened his door, but the annoying notion that something wasn't right persisted, like a dull tooth ache.

Where was Jess? Since his car wasn't in his spot, maybe he'd taken it in for repairs and gotten a ride back. She stopped at his door.

Yesterday's *Evening Post* lay on the floor.

With a shaking finger, she pressed the bell. She had to check on him. What would be the worst thing that could happen? Maybe he'd tell her to take a hike.

The door jerked open, and her heart fell into her stomach. The slender man pushed his glasses up on his nose. "Oh, Mr. Schackelford."

"I thought I heard someone at the door." He wore his usual two day growth of whiskers.

"Wha -- what are you doing here?"

"Oh, you didn't hear? I thought you and Mr. Colton were good friends." He stepped out of the apartment then closed and locked the door.

Holly's heart pounded out of her body. "Hear what?"

"Mr. Colton was rushed to the hospital yesterday. He collapsed at Anderson's Grocery." The apartment manager picked up the *Evening Post* and headed toward the elevators.

Holly trailed the man down the hall, barely keeping pace with his quick steps.

"His sister called and asked me to check his apartment. Mr. Colton won't be returning for quite a while from what I understand. I believe she said he'd be staying at his parents' home when he's released from the hospital." The manager pushed the down button on the elevator.

Blood drained from her head. "Do you know what was wrong? Why he collapsed?"

The doors opened, and he stepped inside the elevator. "What floor do you need?"

"Five, please. Mr. Schackelford, do you know what happened to him?" Holly couldn't restrain the desperation which wrenched her stomach and the rising tone of her voice.

A ding sounded and *five* flashed above the door.

"No, I'm sorry I don't. All I know is he's at Bayview."

The same hospital where his mother had been. Holly stepped out then twirled around, rushing back into the elevator. "I've changed my mind." She glanced up at the panel and punched *Parking Garage.*

~

The brakes on Holly's car screeched as she sped away from the apartment complex. What had happened to Jess? Yesterday when Mr. Schackelford let her in his apartment, she'd suspected a diabetic coma. Could her fears be realized now? *Dear Lord, please take care of him.*

Jess told her to get out of his life. Should she be going to him at the hospital? Her heart told her she could go nowhere else. Even if he didn't want to see her, at least she could sit outside his door and pray.

She parked in the visitors' parking lot. Had it only been a few weeks since she and Jess had come to see his mom and spoken to the woman at the information desk? The same worker staffed the counter. "Jess Colton, please."

The clerk perused her computer screen. "Looks like ICU, ma'am."

Intensive Care Unit. How bad is he?

Holly held her hand to her heart. "Thank you."

"You can access it through that hall." She pointed behind her. "It's in the Bradley Building, but ma'am, they're not going to let you in unless you're a family member." The woman turned back to her computer.

Holly nodded and looped around toward the hall. Family or not, she had to see Jess. She trekked down a long passage, turned right, and plodded through a connecting corridor.

A clerk at the front desk picked up the phone's receiver and scribbled on a piece of paper. Holly slipped by, proceeding down a walkway past the exam rooms. Familiar territory. Her mouth became dry. Especially the room on the right.

She peered into each room as she passed. Close to the end of the hall on her right, she found him. Jess, his face pale, lay in the first bed nearest the wall. An IV ran from his arm, and his eyes were closed. A heart monitor beeped.

"Jess, I'm here." Her words didn't stir him when she moved closer to the bed. No blink, or moan from his lips. Nothing. Jess lay unconscious.

Chapter Fourteen

Holly dared to run her fingers along Jess's hand, careful not to disturb the IV. "This is tearing me apart seeing you like this." She drew a chair beside the bed.

He lay motionless. His chest rose and fell with each breath.

Though he couldn't hear her, she needed to say the words. "I want you to know, no matter what happens, I love you. If you don't love me or for some reason can't find a place for me in your life, it's okay. I just want you to get well." She brushed at the tears rolling down her cheek. "Please, Jess, just get well."

Jess's expressionless face tormented her. Would he regain consciousness? Would she ever talk to him again? The sweet man who thought he had no hope lay vulnerable in a hospital bed.

"Something else you need to know. You are important to God. He sent His only son to die for you. That's how much He loves you. If you don't get better for me, at least get better for God. He's got so much planned for your life. I just know it."

"Excuse me, ma'am." A nurse in a pink scrubs top appeared at the bottom of Jess's bed. "Are you a family member?"

I wish I were. "No, but I'm a close friend." She stood and faced the nurse.

"I'm sorry. You'll have to leave."

"You don't understand. I love this man. I need to stay." The words rushed from her before she gave them a thought.

"Look, I don't make the rules. Now, please, you'll have to leave. If you'll excuse me." The nurse pressed between Holly and the hospital bed. With the stethoscope to her ears, she placed the end on Jess's chest.

"What's going on in here?"

Holly looked from the RN to the woman marching in the room. "Oh, Margaret. I hadn't heard about Jess. Please tell the nurse to allow me to stay."

Her brows dipped between narrowed eyes, and the corners of her mouth curved down. "It's okay, Nurse. I'm the patient's sister. She can stay. We'll be out in a moment anyway."

"All right. Please keep your voices low." She reached to the IV pole to check the drip. After one last glance at Jess, she turned toward the door.

"What happened?" Holly had waited and speculated long enough.

Margaret's eyes mocked her. "You mean you don't know? I thought you two were an item."

This wasn't the time or the place to offer any explanations of her relationship with Jess. "No, I wasn't aware he'd collapsed. The apartment manager told me he'd been taken to Bayview."

Margaret filled her lungs and exhaled. "I guess you'll find out anyway. He's in a diabetic coma. When they brought him in, his blood sugar was close to 600."

"What?" Holly's hand went to her throat. "What do the doctors say?"

"If he doesn't come out of it..." Margaret covered her face. "If he doesn't regain consciousness in another couple of days, chances are he won't make it." Her voice choked. "He could die."

The words ripped through Holly's soul. *Jess could die.* She squeezed back tears and touched Margaret's trembling shoulder. "I love your brother and nothing will keep me from praying for him."

Jess's sister raised tearful eyes to Holly. "I don't know what I'd do if..." She paced to the end of his bed. Then she reeled toward Holly. "Do you really think praying would help him?"

"You know God's word says when two or more agree in prayer about something, it will be done for them. Do you want to pray with me?"

Margaret gazed to the window but nodded.

Holly grasped her hand. With a gentle tug, she pulled her closer to Jess's bedside.

With her other, she touched his shoulder. "Lord, we agree now in prayer. You know how much Jess loves you, and we love him. As his friend and his sister, we ask you to heal him. Bring him back to us from this coma." Whether God chose to heal Jess or not, Holly had to be obedient by praying. "Be merciful to Jess. Help him find control over the things holding him captive. Amen."

"I've never heard anyone pray so personally before." She lowered her head. "I haven't done much praying myself. Thank you." She sat at the end of the bed.

Holly gave Margaret's hand a squeeze. She dropped

her weary body in the chair again.

There seemed little need to converse anymore. Though Jess's white face distressed her, the beeping of the heart monitor reminded her life flowed through him.

Margaret whispered. "How did he get to this place?"

She knew the answer, but she couldn't share this with his sister, especially while he lay in a hospital bed unconscious.

~

Holly stepped out of the elevator at the basement level with Margaret by her side. A sign pointed to the left for the cafeteria. Holly filled her mug from the coffee carafe on the serving line and moved toward the tables. "This okay?"

They slid into a booth for two near the window. Outside in the hospital gardens, bright globes on metal poles lit the dark night.

She held her hand against the hot mug. Though the day had been warm, the heat from the cup comforted her.

"I'm anxious to hear Dr. Van Zant's report when we get back to the room." Margaret took a sip from the thick white ceramic mug. "He certainly shooed us out when he showed up."

"I heard him ask the nurse if there'd been any signs of consciousness. He told her Jess could be moved to the main hospital and out of ICU when he woke up." Time was critical. *Lord, please let it be soon.*

Margaret opened a package of sweetener. "I'm sorry for the way I spoke to you when Mom was in the hospital." She ran her finger around the cup's rim. "I was wrong. I can see how much you care for Jess."

Words she never expected from Margaret. "I appreciate what you're saying, but I don't think he feels the same about me."

"I'm surprised you say that. I know my brother. The way he looks at you -- his face glows like the setting sun." Margaret patted Holly's hand. "I think he loves you."

Could she possibly be right? If Jess loved her, he still didn't want a relationship. "Right now, my only concern is to pray for him to get well." She sipped the last few drops of coffee. "Do you suppose we can go back?"

"I'm ready," she smiled.

Fear shoved its way into Holly's heart again as they stepped out of the elevator to walk the corridor to ICU.

The doctor hovered over Jess when they returned to the room then scribbled something on a clipboard.

"Well, the good news is he's responding to the IV drip. His blood sugar has dropped. He's still comatose, however. Let's hope he comes out of it soon." He glanced at Margaret. "When the time comes, I need to consult with a family member. We will want to get him set up on a strict after-care program."

"Yes, Doctor. Our parents are planning on providing him with at-home supervision."

"Good." The doctor replaced his pin light in his coat pocket and marched toward the door.

Holly pulled up the chair beside his bed and gazed at his pale face. Margaret gripped the rail at the end of the bed and released a sigh. They played a waiting game. Would Jess wake up?

Holly leaned her head back against the wall and closed her eyes.

With a start she sat up. She must've dozed. A glimpse at her watch told her an hour passed since the doctor left. With closed eyes, Margaret leaned back against the chair on the other side of the bed.

The slow rhythm of Jess's breathing quickened, and he coughed.

Holly jumped up and stepped to his side.

Jess's eyes moved under his lids before his lashes fluttered.

Margaret stood and took a few steps toward the bed. "Could it be?" she whispered.

"I don't know." A long breath accompanied Holly's words.

Jess blinked. He rolled his head to Holly and then Margaret. Did they dare hope?

Holly brushed back her tears. He seemed to be coming out of it.

Jess coughed again, and moaned. He lifted his arm attached to the IV. "What? Where… am... I?"

"Shh, Jess. Don't talk now." Holly covered his hand. "You collapsed yesterday at the grocery store. You're at Bayview."

Margaret wiped away a tear, closed the remaining distance between her and Jess, and peered down at him.

He groaned and opened his eyes to Margaret and back at Holly. "I remember. Everything... went black."

"You've been in a coma." Margaret laid her hand on his arm. "You're getting the help you need here at the hospital. Jess, Holly prayed for you." Margaret cried fresh tears, smiling as her gaze fell on Holly. "Thank you. Thank you for praying and being here for him. I'm going to get Mom. She'll be elated." She squeezed Holly's arm. "I believe you're good for him."

Margaret walked toward the door. She slowly turned to Jess and Holly, the corners of her mouth curved up. With a wave, she exited the room.

Jess frowned at Holly. "What are you doing here?" Though his words were almost a whisper, they stung.

~

Jess still didn't want her there. "Would you feel better if I left?"

The IV attached to his hand caught his attention. "I remember how we left things. I'm surprised you'd come."

Holly forced down her frustration. "Jess Colton, you are the most insufferable man. I know what you said, but that doesn't change the fact I love you. I came here to pray for you. Margaret prayed, too."

"Margaret prayed?" He moved his other hand over his forehead.

"Yes, with me." She released a long, slow breath. "I'll leave now because I don't want to do anything to jeopardize your health. Do you mind if I contact Pastor Downing and have someone from church visit you?"

"No." Jess shook his head against the pillow. "Please don't. My problems are no one else's business." His eyes closed, and he moaned.

How could he refuse prayer? Maybe he didn't know what he was saying. "Are you sure?"

Jess's lashes flickered, and he opened his eyes again. His face hardened when he finally looked at her. "Perfectly."

"Then I'll leave now. There's nothing more I can do." Holly rose from the chair and placed her hand on his shoulder. "Good-bye, Jess."

He hadn't changed his mind about her, but if he'd only allow someone to come to the hospital, she'd feel so much better. Once more, she took in his unhappy face and headed out the door. The end had come. She'd never see him again.

"Holly." The weak voice met her ears.

She couldn't read the sick man's expression -- maybe regret, conviction, she wasn't sure.

"Wait, Holly. Come back."

He'd reconsidered, wanted her back in his life. Her emotions soared with joy and fell when she took in his solemn face.

"I don't want to admit it, but I know I need help." He wiped the corner of his eye. "Remember Tim, the youth pastor? He's new to the church. He probably won't be as judgmental." Jess coughed. "Would you ask him to visit?"

Chapter Fifteen

Jess pulled at the IV attached to his hand. How soon would Dr. Van Zant allow him to be free of the thing?

A bitter memory careened through his mind when he recalled how he'd told Holly to leave, but he'd made up his mind before he collapsed. He wouldn't change his decision -- more for her sake than his, even though it ripped his heart apart. He reached behind him to prop his pillow up higher.

When he first woke up, he heard voices from deep within a hole somewhere. Then he opened his eyes and saw Holly's beautiful face looking at him with such compassion and love.

She and Margaret had prayed for him. His sister praying? Now that was a miracle.

Jess pulled the rolling table toward him. He lifted the paper cup to his parched lips. The melted ice soothed his thirst.

"Well, good morning, Mr. Colton." A cheery young woman with short blond hair bounced into his room and wrapped a blood pressure cuff around his arm, then stuck a thermometer in his mouth. She hummed a few bars of some song while she checked his IV. Leaning toward him, she slipped the plastic piece out of his mouth. "Very good."

"When are they going to let me have real food?" He didn't feel a burning hunger, yet his mind told him he needed a meal. All they brought him was beef broth, Jell-O, orange juice, a carton of skim milk, and a cup of decaf coffee with no cream or sugar.

"You'll have to ask your doctor. Sorry I don't know." She pricked his finger and placed a drop of blood on the meter's test strip. "Excellent, your blood sugar is improving." She beamed as she marked the information on a clipboard and opened the window drapes wider. "Well, Mr. Colton, I hope you'll be out of here soon." She turned toward the door but stopped at the threshold.

Dad rushed into the room almost colliding with her.

"Be careful, young lady." He marched past her to the bed.

Jess cringed. Talking to his father was low on his list of priorities right now, but he supposed he didn't have a choice.

"Jess, my boy. I'm sorry you wound up in the hospital." He pulled up a chair and straddled it.

"Yeah, me, too." Jess figured his sudden rise in blood pressure couldn't be good either.

"If you'd followed my instructions, you wouldn't be in here." His dad's deep baritone voice resonated off the walls.

Jess fingered the blanket's soft ribbon. What was the use of answering him? Maybe he should pull the covers over his head.

Dad passed the cup of ice to Jess. "You're a grown man. I don't know why you can't maintain control over your eating habits." He puffed out his chest. "When I was your age, I jogged and played tennis almost every day. You don't know how to take charge of your life. How old do you have to be to finally take responsibility?"

His father's words opened old wounds. As a boy, he never did anything good enough to please him. How many times had Jess run to the backyard and plopped down on the ground with his back against the shed wishing the pain from his dad's cutting words would go away?

Even an advanced degree in computer science hadn't impressed his father. That wasn't enough. Nothing was ever enough.

"Are you listening to me, Jess? When are you finally going to learn to eat like a normal person and stop stuffing yourself?" Dad spewed his hurtful message.

Dizziness overtook Jess. He had no words for his father and fought humiliation. Cry and Dad would be doubly sure his son was a worthless fool.

The clacking of footsteps pulled his attention toward the hall. Mom rushed into the room carrying a paper cup.

"Here's your coffee, John." She thrust a vending machine cup into Dad's hand. "I've always kept my mouth closed, never raised any objections, but the time has come for me to speak up. From the hall I could hear what you said. You have no right to talk to our son like that."

"Marietta, it's for his own good. Jess needs to grow up." He blew on his coffee.

Mom's brows formed a V. Jess had never seen her

so angry. "Listen to me. Our son needs support and love right now." She gave a quick glance at Jess before turning a furious gaze to Dad. "If we'd lost him, how would you feel if the last words he heard from you came with condemnation?"

Dad straightened. Coffee splattered to the floor. The thought of his parents in his hospital room arguing over him became unbearable. "Mom, it's all right." A strong thirst overpowered him.

She spun to Jess. "No honey. It's not." As if to protect him, she moved to the head of his bed. "My, poor baby. I'm sorry about what he said to you." She straightened his covers.

"Marietta, just stop it." Dad drained the remaining coffee and tossed the cup in the garbage can. "He's not a boy any more. You're treating him like one."

A wave of nausea passed through Jess's stomach. "Mom, Dad. I'm not feeling well. I'd like to try to get some sleep. Would you mind leaving me alone?"

Mom placed her hand on her waist. "Now see what you've done."

If Jess was going to pass out again, this would be a good place for it -- in a hospital bed. "I'm not blaming anyone."

"You need to tell our son you're sorry." She pushed back a few strands of hair on Jess's head.

Would you stop mothering me?

Dad's voice boomed louder. "I don't need your advice."

A nurse poked her head in the door. "Is everything all right in here? I'm sorry, but I'm going to have to ask you to lower your voices."

"Oh, shut up." Dad's rudeness embarrassed Jess.

"I'm leaving." His father stormed out of the room.

Jess's brain continued to swirl. He needed to sleep, or better yet, he needed a bacon double cheeseburger.

"Honey, I'll be back tomorrow with Margaret. I'm sorry your father chastised you." She kissed his cheek and left.

Jess laid his head back and counted the ceiling tiles. Was there some way he could bribe a nurse to get him some fried chicken, or even tacos? Better yet, an ice cream sundae. How much money would it take?

~

The sun shone bright through the hospital window. Jess didn't remember much from last night. He'd decided against bribery and asked for something to help him sleep. The medication the nurse slipped into his IV knocked him out.

He almost cheered when the morning nurse took him off the IV. She said he no longer needed the hydration since his sugar levels were stable. Dr. Van Zant would either switch him to the main hospital or send him home this morning. Jess couldn't wait to be in charge of his life again.

Maybe he should ring the nurse's station and ask them when he'd get breakfast. He craved a cup of coffee with cream and sugar. Maybe some bacon and eggs.

Dad walked into the room. "Hello, Jess."

Jess's shoulders dropped to his knees. He was trapped with no way of escape. "Hello, Dad. If you've come to scold me, could you at least wait until they give me breakfast -- probably a piece of wheat bread, some cottage cheese or oatmeal, skim milk, and a banana? The diabetic food in this hospital is just scrumptious." Jess didn't bother to restrain his sarcasm.

An expression crossed his father's face, one Jess hadn't seen before. "I came to check on you. What'd the doctor say?" Dad sat in the chair beside the bed.

"He hasn't been in this morning, but I'm ready to go home." Anywhere would be better than here under his father's scrutiny.

"No." Dad shook his head. "You're coming to stay with us."

Was that a command? Well, he wasn't about to obey. He needed a safe haven from his father. "I'm going home to my apartment."

Dad squared his jaw. "You need someone to take care of you, to make sure you eat the right food."

"Please. I can't talk about this right now." No way would he allow his parents to look after him. Pain mounted in Jess's stomach. Where was his breakfast? Would whipped cream on strawberries be out of the question?

As if feeling sorry for his words, Dad studied his hands. "You're right. I didn't come here to beat up on you."

Maybe he could distract Dad from remembering what an idiot he had for a son. "How's work going?"

"Fine, Jess, fine, but I didn't come here to discuss my work either." A muscle in his jaw twitched.

Jess inhaled a deep breath and rubbed at an ache developing in his temples.

His father's eyes bored down on him. "You know I care for you, don't you?"

His mouth fell open. "What?"

"Well, maybe with all my railing against you, I

don't communicate it very well, but I've always cared about you."

"I know that. You've always provided for Margaret and me. We've never lacked for anything in our lives."

"I'd like to think I have, but providing to the best of our abilities -- that's what fathers are supposed to do. Caring for you -- loving you -- that comes from our hearts."

Jess struggled to sit up.

Dad got to his feet and situated the pillows, then sat back down. "I thought a lot about how I left things yesterday." He smiled. "Of course, a stern lecture, the likes of which I've never received from your mother, persuaded me a bit."

They didn't have to go there. "Dad, I--"

"Let me finish." He raised a hand to silence him. "I know I come off as a know-it-all on occasion."

"On occasion?" Jess's eye twitched. Where was Dad going with this?

"Maybe I don't know everything. I certainly haven't been able to make my son realize how much I care." His eyes misted over. "Despite all my bluster, I'm proud of you. Your mom hit home when she asked how I'd feel if you died without hearing a word of encouragement from me." Dad stood and clasped a hand on Jess's shoulder. "Can you forgive me for my harsh words?"

Jess nodded and cleared his throat of emotion. "There's nothing to forgive. It's just your way."

Taking a step backward, Dad clasped the edges of the windowsill as if to hold him up. "I suppose you haven't heard many encouraging words from me in the past."

What did his father want him to say? Words he didn't have the strength to offer. "Mom must've got on you in a big way."

"Yes, she did, but your mother helped me realize we could've lost you. And my only son wouldn't know I loved him."

The pounding in Jess's head lessened. He couldn't remember the last time Dad said he loved him. Leaning over the bed, his father gave him a hug and patted his shoulder. "We've got to concentrate on you getting better. Then we'll work on us."

"I feel better already." He gripped his father's hand, the apology mending a few of the broken pieces of Jess's spirit.

Chapter Sixteen

Jess's room on the third floor of the main building didn't look much different than the one in ICU. At least he wasn't attached to the IV. Thank the Lord the shots of insulin were temporary until his levels became more stable. When he left the hospital, he'd control his diabetes with medication. But the doctor's decision came with a stipulation -- lose weight. Could he do something he'd failed at every time in the past?

Dr. Van Zant's edict yesterday to keep Jess in the hospital for a few more days disappointed him. He clenched his teeth. The severity of his condition dawned on him. How had he allowed himself to get to this point? Yet, even now, he could've eaten three of the meals they brought at breakfast.

Memories of his father's visit last evening soared through his head. It seemed unreal. They'd made a strong start to a new relationship. Praise God for that.

Slowly, the anticipation of good health became more of a possibility. He picked up the Bible Margaret brought from home and turned to Psalms.

His life as a computer geek, his apartment, even Woodlyn. Did Jess want to return to all that?

Before his collapse, his career had been important

to him. Now he wasn't sure.

Jess flipped through a few pages of Psalms. He had a lot of time to think. What did he want to do with the rest of his life?

He stopped. God had given him so much. Education, his career, a family. Holly. He'd been willing to throw them all away. For what? Food?

"Good morning, sir." A teenage girl in jeans and navy-blue tee shirt with *Bayview Hospital* embroidered on the pocket bounced into the room. She pushed a cart filled with reading materials.

"How ya doing?"

"Great. Would you like a book or magazine?" A rubber wrist band on her arm said *Get Fit Woodlyn*.

"How about a magazine on fitness?" If he was to embrace the gifts God provided, if he wanted to truly become the man Holly deserved, he'd best learn how to take care of himself. He'd known these facts before, but until he'd faced the possibility of death, he hadn't allowed them to truly penetrate his mind.

The girl searched one side of the cart thumbing through the periodicals and books. "*Health and Fitness.* Here you go." She raised the magazine out of the pile and placed it on his table. "Will that be all?"

"Yes, thanks."

"Have a nice day, sir." With a wave, she rolled the cart out of the room.

Jess gave her a thumbs up and flipped open the magazine. The first article featured a story on the need to eat. That was right up his wide alley. The article went on to describe how six small meals a day, a combination of carbohydrates, protein, and fat could keep a person from overindulgence, and work to reduce his weight. Weight would come off faster with an exercise regime.

Sounded easy, but Jess had attempted this diet before and look where it got him.

The wall clock said over two hours until they brought the lunch tray. Maybe he'd doze. He closed the publication and pushed it to one side. A book lay on the table. Must've been under the magazine.

He turned it over and back again. Hmm. *God Is on Your Side -- A Spiritual Guide to Overcoming the Power of Sin.* An interesting title.

Since he hadn't asked for it, how did get here? Did the Holy Spirit put it in his path? Jess shrugged. Maybe God wanted him to read it.

~

Lunch of dry chicken and rice, green beans, a cup of fruit, and a container of Jell-O had come and gone. Hey, maybe if he ate this all the time, he'd lose weight. It'd be so tasteless he wouldn't gorge on the stuff. The scrap of paper in the book *God Is on Your Side* marked chapter fifteen -- where he'd left off.

Jess took a gulp of ice water and focused on the page. A self-help book had never been on his list of favorites. Yet the more he read, the more the message spoke to him. He'd been forgiven, but now as a Christian, what hold did sin have over him?

The Word said the power of sin died with Christ on the cross. The scripture from Proverbs spoke of gluttony, and it still had power over him.

Wasn't he free of sin? A verse in Romans reached out and grabbed him. We are no longer slaves to sin. He didn't have to be a slave to gluttony.

He laid his head back on the pillow and took a deep breath. *Lord, is that possible for me? All things are possible with God.* He liked this line of thinking.

A knock sounded, and he looked toward the door. A young man with spiky brown hair -- Tim Garrett. "Hi, Jess. Are you up for a visit?"

Jess scooted up in bed. "Hey, Tim. Sure. Come in."

Tim flashed him a huge grin as he stepped inside and pulled up a chair. "Your friend, Holly, called me a couple of days ago. I'm sorry this is the soonest I could get here." He laid his Bible in his lap. "Those young people are keeping me going."

"I certainly understand if you don't have the time." The man probably concerned himself mainly with teens.

"I have plenty of time for you."

"Yeah, well, I'm honored you'd leave work to see me. I haven't been fifteen for quite a while, and right now I'm feeling a lot older than my thirty-two years."

"Hey, buddy. I'm sorry you're not feeling well. Holly said you've been diagnosed with diabetes. She's pretty worried about you."

"Holly's a nice person." What else could he say?

"Well, don't tell her I said so, but I get the idea she's more than a little fond of you."

Jess pinched the bridge of his nose. "I'd just as soon not talk about Holly right now."

"Hey, man. I apologize." Tim opened his Bible and thumbed through a few pages.

The guy was new to ministry, probably not sure what to say. "Look, buddy. I'm sorry. It's just Holly and I... we..."

Tim ran a hand through his hair. "Forget it. I just came here to cheer you up and share the Word if I could."

Somehow he sensed this man had the answers he needed. Jess's heart pounded as faith renewed within him. He could trust Tim.

Jess met his gaze. "I need help. I may see the Lord face to face sooner than I thought if things don't change."

Tim sat straighter in his chair and stared at Jess. Then a slow smile spread across his face. "I love a challenge."

~

"I don't know when I've drunk so much water." Jess laughed. "It's a lot better than stuffing my stomach with food." Jess thanked the Lord he'd asked Holly to call Tim, even though he wondered what she told the youth pastor about their relationship.

The nurse's assistant brought another pitcher of water and two cups. Tim poured one for Jess and another for himself. "Here you go." He set Jess's cup on his bed table.

Tim cleared his voice. "Tell me how I can help you."

"Shall I lay it out for you without sparing words?" Jess slapped his hand against his stomach.

Tim nodded, maintaining a steady gaze.

"I'm a glutton." There. Jess stated the facts. Just by doing so, another piece of his broken life fit into place. He gave a deep sigh. The look of compassion on Tim's face amazed him.

"By saying it, you've taken the first step." The corners of Tim's mouth lifted. "But gluttony is a symptom of something else. I'd like for us to explore that."

Jess suspected his family relationships played a part. But was there an even deeper cause?

"You know, the world would say all you need to do is replace your unhealthy diet with nutritious foods and proper exercise."

"Yeah. This article in *Health and Fitness* said as much." He held up the magazine.

Tim nodded. "Oh, don't get me wrong. That's a step you need to take, but you're going to fail."

Jess swallowed. Tim didn't know him at all and even he could see the facts. Jess didn't have what it took to get his life back.

A slow smile crossed Tim's face. "You need to give Jesus control of your life."

"It's not like I haven't tried in the past. I used to drink and did something under the influence that I regretted later. I leaned on Jesus, and I walked away from alcohol. Thing is, I replaced it with another addiction -- food."

"Man is a slave to whatever he allows to master him. First alcohol, now the overuse of food has you in its clutches. But there is freedom because your old self was crucified with Jesus." Tim scratched his head. "Look, man. don't you think the Lord wants you to enjoy good health?"

"Yeah, sure, that makes sense."

"On top of that, if you give Him a chance, God will strengthen you with His power. He'll give you the support you need for the change in diet, exercise, and lifestyle." Tim held up his Bible. "You said you replaced alcohol with food, and that's where you got yourself into trouble. Why not replace both with God this time."

Jess paused, taking in Tim's words. "I've prayed so many times to be free."

"Have you first confessed this as sin and admitted to God you're powerless over your addiction?"

Sin. He wasn't sure he like that word. "No, not like that."

"Listen, my brother. This is a spiritual problem. Hang on to God's power and appropriated it in your life."

Jess found no words for Tim. The magnitude of his emotions didn't allow them. For the first time, he had true hope that he could be free.

Tim grinned. "I can see you understand what I'm saying. Let's pray."

"You got it." Jess blinked back a tear he hoped Tim didn't see.

Tim placed his hand on Jess's shoulder, bowed his head, and closed his eyes. He prayed for Jess's release from the chains binding him. Then he begged God to help him be a friend to Jess. When he finished, he asked, "Why don't you offer up a prayer?"

Jess swallowed hard. "Dear Lord." He paused. "I've felt so distant from you for so long now. I was afraid you'd take away the only thing giving me comfort. I didn't stop to realize You are my comfort. I didn't seek You in my pain. I didn't come to You as my heavenly Father when the hurts of my earthly father were too much for me to bear. I didn't trust You."

He glanced up to find Tim's head bowed and

nodding in agreement. "Lord, I didn't trust You to take away the cravings for things I shouldn't reach for and to give me the things that will truly delight my heart. Your love. My dad's love. Holly's love. Well, Lord, I'm trusting You now. In Jesus Name. Amen."

Tim's head remained bowed, his eyes closed. Then he raised his gaze to Jess. "Praise God. What a beautiful prayer." He stood and stretched. "If it's okay with you, I'd like to continue to meet when you get out of the hospital."

"You bet, buddy. For as long as you're willing to put up with me." Jess lowered his head and studied his hands. "I could use a good, objective friend."

"If you'll give me your key and your permission to go into your kitchen, I'll clear out any unhealthy food and fill your cabinets with nutritious items."

"Are you serious?" Jess's mouth fell open. "That would be awesome. Look, I'll give you some cash for a couple of trips to the grocery store."

Tim walked to the end of the bed. "I'm not trying to intrude on your life. This is just to help you out until you get back on your feet. After Holly mentioned your hospital stay was diabetes related, I rounded up a few secret chefs to make meals for a while. I'd like you to commit to eating only what they bring until you get into the habit of eating healthy, and feel you can do it on your own. I want to be an accountability partner for you."

Jess had become entirely too emotional since he'd been in the hospital. He swiped at a tear on his cheek. He didn't speak, couldn't trust his voice in the wake of the goodness of his church family. He raised his eyes to Tim and nodded. Finally he found his voice. "Thanks, buddy."

~

Holly eased down on her couch. She loved working with Dr. Murphy, but today her knee hurt. She laid her head back on the couch pillow and closed her eyes. The ache in her knee dissolved as Jess's handsome face flooded her mind. He'd been released from the hospital today, and Tim said he'd bring him home.

Though her heart ached to see him, she wouldn't compromise his recovery -- whatever it took. She'd resigned herself to the fact she might never have a relationship with him. He'd banished her from his life.

The temporary food plan she and Tim had talked about seemed great. Whether she'd ever see Jess again or not, she desired with all her heart to help out. She volunteered for breakfast every morning. An easy task. Drop it off in front of his door, ring the doorbell, and walk away. Since Jess's apartment wasn't as far from the elevators and the stairs as hers, she could disappear quickly, and he'd never know it was her. She agreed with Tim Jess should recuperate at his apartment instead of his parents' house. Maybe he'd even get a little work done.

Where was her future headed? Would she ever marry and have the child her heart desired? She couldn't see herself with anyone except Jess, but they were over. God had something else in store for her.

Chapter Seventeen

Jess rose from his computer and stretched. His mind revved on overload. Out the window of his home office, gray skies blended with the soaked sidewalks and streets. Dead leaves covered the ground. Hard to believe he'd been out of the hospital for six weeks. He rounded his lips and exhaled a long breath.

The bathroom scales gave him a good report this morning. Since his hospital stay he'd lost thirty-five pounds. The first stride up a tall mountain.

Thanks to Tim's visits and the delicious food the secret chefs at church delivered to his door three times a day for several weeks, he saw progress. Most of the people would ring his doorbell and wait for him to answer to pass him a delicious meal. Unlike his breakfast deliveries, where someone rang the bell and left the meal before he could answer.

Now the responsibility of his nutrition rested on his shoulders. Weight Watchers Online helped, but everything they taught him, he already knew. His problem wasn't in knowing what to do, but in doing it. He relaxed when he thought of his good visit to Dr. Van Zant's office.

During Tim's faithful meetings, Jess understood

more and more. The root of his problem was sin. He'd allowed his gluttonous behavior to reign, shutting out the truth of God's Word, refusing to admit the depth of his failings. Delving into the Bible became the key to his slow progress.

Jess strolled into the kitchen and opened the fridge. He pulled a bottle of water out of the side door. More than once, he'd fought the urge to binge since he'd returned home. A couple of times, he had to pray and call Tim. It helped having his kitchen clear of the trigger foods. Now when he shopped for groceries, he stuck with a strict list, buying only those items he needed from his pre-planned menus.

Tim's help was invaluable, guiding him in understanding the roots of his addictive personality which were grounded in his dysfunctional family. Though he'd been injured by his father, Jess had turned to food and not the Lord for comfort, yet he couldn't blame anyone for his behavior. As an adult, he had to take control over his life

He drifted back to the window. The deciduous trees were bare, but the beautiful evergreens retained their color year round. One thing he liked about the Seattle area, during fall and winter, one could look out and still see greenery.

The gardens were visible down below. His heart pounded when he thought of the times he and Holly sat in the swing, and the moment he'd kissed her. Once, she'd walked past him in the lobby. He smiled but didn't stop to talk. He sensed her gaze on him as he moved away toward the elevators. His heart told him to call her, but he wasn't ready, not until he knew he'd conquered his addiction. The day would come when he would be free to pick up the phone and ask her if they still had a chance. Right now, though, he had to take things one step at a time.

From the seventh floor, the walkways and road beyond the apartment grounds appeared dark with moisture. Umbrellas popped up everywhere this time of year. The Douglas firs dripped huge drops of water onto the grass.

He lifted his gaze to the sky. The gray clouds of fall and winter no longer depressed him. He'd lived here long enough to be used to it. His image in the window reflected a smile on his face. The joy inside of him came from knowing that with God he could experience victory.

Things worked out well. Jim understood the delay in his project because of Jess's stint in the hospital. Vauxhall actually put the project on hold awhile anyway to settle a labor dispute. The Lord had greatly blessed him. Jess neared the end of the project, satisfied with his performance despite the road bumps.

Wherever he journeyed from here, God would be the one to direct his steps. Pastor Downing's messages still spoke to him. He laughed at the gang of ragtag teenagers Tim and Jess sat with every week. Each Sunday he looked around for Holly but never saw her, though he wouldn't know what to do if he did. Since Woodlyn Fellowship only had one service, it became obvious she'd stopped coming. Jess's heart ached with the knowledge. Had he caused his Christian sister to stumble?

Time to get back to work. He strolled into the kitchen and took an apple out of the fridge. The slices of the juicy fruit tasted delicious spread with low fat peanut butter -- a hint from Weight Watchers. He'd work for three more hours before heading to the apartment gym. Wasn't he ready for the next step? A better gym with more equipment? Diana's gym.

~

Jess pushed on the double glass doors of Sound Fitness. He wasn't prepared for what he saw in front of him. A sea of exercise equipment filled the enormous room. Treadmills, stationary bikes, machines with pulleys, elliptical steppers, rowers, and other similar torture devices were arranged in circular patterns.

An athletic-looking young woman perched on a stool behind the front desk to his left. "Yes, sir. May I help you?"

He might've been the only chubby person in the place. His baggie gray sweats hid some of his rolls of fat. "Yes, I'd like to speak to Diana if she's here. I don't have an appointment, but please tell her Jess Colton would like to talk with her about a membership."

The girl glanced at her computer and back at him. "Sir, we've got several associates who can assist you."

"I know, but I'd like to see Diana." She'd invited him to the gym in the first place.

The perky woman's blond ponytail bounced as she turned toward an office behind her desk. A plaque on the door read *Diana Harkins*. Miss Perky knocked then entered, shutting the door behind her. Not more than thirty seconds later, Diana walked out. Her bicycle shorts and athletic top highlighted her trim body. A wide-eyed glance changed to a smile.

With an extended hand, she marched around the

counter. "Well, hello, Jess. I'm glad to see you. I hope you made the decision to join us."

"I'm here for a transformation. It's about time, wouldn't you say?" He chuckled.

Diana grinned. "You've come to the right place, and it looks like you've lost some weight. Good job. Tell you what. I usually don't do this, but I'm going to be your personal trainer. No extra charge, since you're a friend of Holly's." She winked.

"Thanks. My remaining flab is all yours." If anybody could motivate him, it had to be Diana.

She pointed to the elliptical machine. "Go ahead. Get on." She didn't show an ounce of mercy.

Jess placed his feet on the pedals and started moving.

"I'm going to increase the incline and speed it up a little." She reached her finger to the display window between the handle bars. "You can do it."

One thing about Diana, she explained what he was doing and why. Jess tried to breathe through his nose and exhale through his mouth. A towel caught the moisture when he wiped his forehead. Finally, the timer dinged.

"Okay, Jess. You can stop. That was fifteen minutes."

"O... kay." Jess puffed. "Can... I rest... for a minute?"

Diana gave him a quick grin. "All right. I'll give you a break this time."

He stepped off the machine and strained to pull air into his lungs. He bent down and placed his hands on his knees catching another breath. His heart didn't pound quite as fast now. "Whew."

"Let's try some weights."

A bench faced a mirrored wall. From the sound of the grunts and groans around him, he was in for a tough workout with the hand-held pieces of metal."

Diana placed a twenty pound black bar in each hand. "Now you're going to extend your lower arms out and back bending at the elbow. Do as many reps as you comfortably can."

"Ugh." Jess joined the chorus of moans.

"Good. That was ten. Now grip the bars and push straight up in the air, and bring them back down. Do ten of those."

Jess's arms were ready to drop off. "Please... tell me... we're finished with this." He shoved the weights one last time into the air.

"Okay, you can sit up and rest for a minute."

He huffed a few more times and looked at Holly's sister hovering over him. "I appreciate... your personal attention." He struggled for another breath. "You and Holly both have such a... giving nature."

She stared at the floor. "Yeah, but we don't think alike on a lot of issues."

Breathing got easier with a few more deep breaths. "I suppose you mean... about God."

She folded her arms over her chest. "I see you've been talking to her."

"We've shared our opinions, yes." He stood and replaced the weights in the holder. "I think Holly believes... like I do." He forced in another breath. "We recognize our blaring faults."

"Yeah, but it's no fun admitting them."

"I know, but when we do, God... doesn't turn away from us."

Diana's eyes were wide as if his words surprised her.

"He still loves us and wants to forgive." He took another breath.

"I always thought you had to be perfect to please God."

"Just the opposite." Jess wiped his brow. "When we're helpless, He's strong."

"Holly said the same thing, but it was harder to hear it from her. Like she was pointing her finger at me. Coming from you seems easier."

"You're right. It is easier to hear it from someone not so close to you." Jess glanced at the burly guy lifting a fifty-pound weight. "I'd be in trouble if we had to be perfect before God loved us."

Diana tucked a strand of hair behind her ear. "You mean I don't have to find a way to make up for the wrong things I did?"

"You could never do that." He reached down to refasten the Velcro on his shoe and puffed, his stomach cutting off his breath.

"This one is easy." She led him to the upright bike. "All you have to do is peddle. Of course, I'm going to increase your resistance after awhile."

The bike's seat supported his weight. "It's like this. When I come to the gym, I have to work hard to have a trim body. But it's different with God. There's nothing I can do to make myself right. He does it all."

She put her hands on her waist and fixed him with a firm stare. "What really brought you here today?"

He peddled a slow pace. "Up until a few months ago, I was a mess even though I had God in my life. I hadn't let Him take control. I overate yet I knew it was wrong." He breathed a little faster.

"God didn't condemn you for it?" Her gaze studied him.

"No, not in the sense I think you mean. He allowed me to live with the consequences." Jess kept his steady, unhurried speed. "I went into a diabetic coma and..." He gripped the handlebars. "I got out of the hospital six weeks ago. I see now what I was doing to myself. God made a way for me when I gave Him control."

"The way you talk about Him, I can almost believe God is kind and not some deity sitting in the sky ready to strike me down." Diana cast her eyes to the floor, then back up to him. "So God doesn't hold anything against Holly?"

He pressed harder on the pedals. "God doesn't... whew... remember the wrong things... we do anymore when we ask Him... whew... to forgive us."

"Diana, please come to the front desk." A voice blared over the intercom.

She glanced toward the gym's entrance and back at him. "Is it the same with me?"

Jess shaped an O with his lips and blew out as he increased the speed. "It can be..." He wiped his brow. "You have to ask Him first... whew." He smiled though each word came with an effort.

"I'm supposed to be helping you get fit." She tossed her hair off her forehead. "I think you've helped me with another kind of fitness. Religious fitness."

"Maybe... spiritual conditioning." Jess slowed for the cool down.

Diana turned her attention to the front desk. "You've given me a lot to think about. Can we talk again the next time you come in?"

"Absolutely. Thank you for the workout." He grinned at her. "I'll sign a contract and pay my membership before I leave."

Her gaze lingered on him a moment longer then she turned toward the main entrance.

Jess wiped his brow and stepped off the bike. A few more machines and he'd hit the shower at home. Who knew? He'd humbled himself to seek help from Diana, and God had used him to draw her closer to His Kingdom.

JUNE FOSTER

Chapter Eighteen

The lines and symbols on Jess's computer screen held him captive. He squared his shoulders. He approached the end of the project and in his opinion, Vauxhall would benefit from the new application. His pocket buzzed so he stuffed his hand into his loose-fitting jeans and pulled out his phone. "Jess Colton."

"Jess, this is Jim. How are you doing?"

After six sessions with Diana in the last two weeks, he felt better about himself. "Fine, Jim." He took a deep breath. "I'm feeling positive about the project." *And my health.*

"You have every right. Management is pleased with your weekly reports. Say, Jess. In order to implement the application for Vauxhall, Mr. Zimmerman wants us to make arrangements to send you to Ellesmere. Provide instruction, hands on help, that kind of thing. The stint will be for no less than three months, maybe four. Are you up to it?"

Jess put his phone on speaker, set it down on his desk, and walked to the window. Was he ready? Was his eating under control enough to make the trip? Could he be apart from Tim, his accountability partner, for that long?

He lived in the age of computers. He could follow Weight Watchers Online anywhere and stay in touch with Tim by e-mail or even Skype. And the Lord? The Lord would travel with him to the ends of the earth.

"Jess, are you there?"

"Sorry, Jim. Just thinking. When should I expect to leave?"

"Is your passport current?"

"Per Evergreen policy. Yes, sir."

"Good. You leave in three days."

~

Holly turned off her coffeemaker and washed her cup. The church had stopped sending meals some time ago, but Tim said Jess had managed on his own under Tim's supervision -- something about following Weight Watchers Online.

She prayed for Jess daily, more than daily. Every time she thought of him, like every other minute.

Jogging became impossible for her on the Evergreen Woodland Trail unless she wanted to carry an umbrella and skirt mud puddles. Even then, she couldn't avoid tramping through pools of murky water. She hated to admit she hadn't worked out since Tim brought Jess home from the hospital, and she'd prepared breakfast for him every morning.

Her Bible, still on the kitchen table, lay open to the Psalms after this morning's reading. She loved Jess and wanted nothing more than for him to come back into her life, but she had to give him the space he needed. Maybe he wanted it this way. Maybe he didn't care for her anymore, or maybe he'd found someone else.

Slipping down to the table, she thumbed through her Bible. An old bulletin from Woodlyn Fellowship caught her attention. She missed the congregation, but it was better for Jess if she didn't attend. Since Marcela had invited her to go to Faith Temple, it seemed a good option. She liked their preacher but missed Pastor Downing.

Lacing her fingers together, she stretched her arms out. If she didn't get some exercise soon, her body would protest. But in Western Washington this time of year, the only choice was the gym. She'd be welcomed at Diana's place of business, and her sister never charged her membership dues.

Holly changed to sweats and her jogging leg then grabbed her gym bag and turned the knob on the front door.

Ring.

Never failed. Her phone chirped when she had her hands full. She considered not answering but backed into the apartment and set her purse down, pulling her cell from the little outside pocket. "Hello."

"Holly, this is Margaret. How are things going with you?" Her voice carried a note of apprehension.

A knot formed in her stomach. The thought of talking to Jess's sister made her nervous. What if she asked about their relationship? "Oh, same as everyone else. I'm trying to stay dry."

"I wanted to let you know, I still think of you. I haven't seen you in a while."

"Yeah, same here." Margaret's words encouraged her. Yet Holly didn't totally trust her. Why had she called?

Margaret cleared her throat. "Your prayer that

evening, your prayer for Jess, it meant something to me. For the first time in my life, I sensed God is real."

As if she'd already been to the gym, Holly's heart pounded. Margaret sounded sincere. "He is. Your brother helped me with that realization."

"I haven't seen Jess lately. I know he's been busy with work." She paused. "I went to his apartment the other day to check on him, and he's doing pretty well on his diet. He's losing weight."

Hmm. Now she suspected Margaret knew of their rift. *Why else would she tell me this?* "Yeah, a bunch of people at church helped him out for a while."

"He didn't mention you. I'm being nosy, but do you two still see each other?"

She knows. "Not right now. Jess needs time to himself, to get his life in order."

"Then I guess you haven't heard."

Margaret, get to the point. "Heard what?"

"He's fine, but he left for England yesterday to finish up the project he's working on. He'll be there for a number of months."

The phone slipped from Holly's hand and fell on the floor with a thud. In a hidden place in her heart, she always thought she'd run into him, maybe in the lobby or the elevator, somewhere. He'd smile at her, seeking her friendship or even love. She hoped if they could just talk awhile, or go for a walk under an umbrella, or even meet at their swing, a door would open for them. Now the little bit of optimism Holly clung to died.

Chapter Nineteen

Holly took the last sip of coffee and switched off the pot on her counter in the kitchen where she'd made breakfast for Jess all those weeks. She fought the desire to take the elevator to the seventh floor, to the door where she'd delivered the meals. He wasn't there, but being near his apartment for a moment...

How silly. Once she had the audacity to believe that a day would come when she'd make meals for him on a permanent basis. Now the chances of that looked bleak.

She strolled to her window. The incessant rain beat down on the sidewalks below. Christmas and New Year had come and gone. Hard to believe Jess had been in England for two months.

Saturday mornings were lonely now. Maybe she'd turn on the gas logs in the fireplace and catch up on her reading. The latest Joy Massenburge novel lay on her coffee table.

A muffled ring sounded from her purse. She turned from the living room to the entry table and stuck her fingers in the outside pocket, always cherishing the hope it might be Jess. She snapped the phone open and placed it to her ear. "Hello."

"Hey." Diana greeted her for once with a pleasant

tone.

"If you're calling about going jogging, it's a bit soggy on the trail."

"No, I don't want to run. I wondered if you'll be at home for a while. I'd like to talk to you."

"Well, sure." She strolled back into the kitchen. "I'll put on another pot of coffee."

The aromatic grounds filled the paper filter then water from the reservoir dribbled down sending an earthy aroma to her nose. Her open Bible on the kitchen table beckoned. She needed the strength she'd find in the book of Psalms. The day was gloomy enough. Holly sighed.

"Why are you downcast, O my soul? Why so disturbed within me? Put your hope in God, for I will yet praise him, my Savior and my God." Putting her hope in God and praising Him. That's what He wanted of her. If she never saw Jess Colton again, she'd always praise and hope in her Savior.

The doorbell dinged. She pushed up from the table and stepped forward with her right leg, allowing her better balance. The chain remained attached when she pulled the door open a couple of inches.

Diana stood on the other side. Holly released the security lock and opened the door wide. "Come in. Is it freezing outside?"

"Not too bad." Diana took off her coat and dropped it on a chair in the living room. She parked herself on the couch. "Come sit down." She patted the seat beside her.

How bad would this lecture be?

Diana pinned her with a penetrating look. "I don't know if you're still seeing Jess or not."

"I don't want to talk about him now, but I might as well tell you. I'm not seeing him. In fact, he's in England and will be for quite a while." Her sister's intentions were worse than she'd thought. Diana wanted to berate her about Jess again.

"Oh?" She looked at Holly with big eyes. "I guess that's why he hasn't been to the gym. Maybe he did mention something about his trip the last time he worked out."

"The last time he what? Jess went to your gym to exercise?"

"Yes, he was coming in regularly until the end of November." Diana fingered the fringe on her vest. "That's what I wanted to talk to you about. A lot of what Jess and I discussed has changed my beliefs. I have a new understanding of God."

Holly's hand moved to her mouth. "You talked to Jess about God -- at the gym?"

"Yes. He's helped me to understand so much." Diana stood and strolled to the window. She whirled around to gaze at Holly. "I'm sorry for all these years I told you God couldn't forgive you. I had no idea who He really is." Diana sat back down on the couch and reached for Holly's hand. "I'm so sorry. You were right, and I was deceived. Can you forgive me?"

She could hardly believe her sister's words. "Of course I'll forgive you, but you mean this came about from your conversations with Jess?" Her emotions played tug-a-war in her chest. On one hand, she was overjoyed to hear about the change in Diana, but Jess had accomplished this without her. He'd gone to the gym, spent time with Diana, and never told her. She strangled her emotions.

"I worked with him as a personal trainer, and we had a lot of time to talk. He helped me to understand humans can't do anything to save themselves. God did it all for us. I was so wrong about you." A wistful smile fell across her face. "I used to think I was better in God's eyes, but I see how mistaken I was."

Holly's mouth remained open with the impact of Diana's message. "I'm so happy to hear it." Despite Holly feelings, God had used Jess. She lowered her head, her words a whisper. "I love you, Diana."

"I love you too, and I'm so sorry for what you've been through in the past. I want to spend my time being the sister you didn't have before." She embraced Holly. "I pray God will open up the door for you to marry that handsome lug of a guy."

Holly pulled from her sister's hold. "I'm still in love with him, and I hope the day comes when we'll be married, but there's not a lot I can do to make it happen. God has to bring us together.

"Come here, girl. I'm going to pray He does." Diana grabbed her hand again.

"I didn't know you believed in praying."

"I do now."

~

Holly set the little valentine card on Marcela's desk next to her phone. *Hallmark* cards said it best. Holly laughed at the cute bear with hearts popping out of his chest. The message, "Love bears all things," matched the picture. She slipped back into her cubicle to check her schedule for the day. Her next patient wasn't for twenty minutes.

Time had slowed since Jess left. Sometimes her days seemed empty, but little by little, her heart relinquished the hope of ever seeing him again. She even allowed Marcela to convince her to go out with her brother. The guy was a sweet Christian man, but after three dates, he hadn't called her again. Probably because he sensed her disinterest.

Her phone rang. She dug her purse out of her cabinet and rifled through the pockets. She pulled the phone out and ambled to the window overlooking busy College Boulevard. Until the month of June, they wouldn't see any change in the gray, overcast skies. "Hello."

"Holly, this is Jess."

Her heart stopped. She braced herself with a hand against the window. "How are you?" The struggle to keep her voice steady defied her.

"Good, Holly, good." He cleared his throat.

Maybe this phone call challenged him as well.

"It's been awhile since we've talked."

He didn't have to tell her that. She knew how long, almost to the day. "Are you home?"

"No, I'm still in Ellesmere, England."

What possible motive would he have to call? "Margaret told me you were working there for a while."

"Holly, I'm sorry I didn't tell you goodbye. Things were--"

She shot her gaze toward the ceiling. "That's fine, Jess. You owe me no explanation. I'm glad to hear you're okay."

"Yes, thank the Lord. Look, Holly. I'm coming home next week." He paused.

"Okay." She bit her lower lip. The man left without

telling her, and now he thought he should inform her of his return?

"Am I catching you at a bad time?" he asked.

She needed to give him the benefit of the doubt here. "No, I'm between patients. How are things?"

"You mean have I gone into another diabetic coma?"

"No, Jess. I trust you to take care of yourself. I just meant your health."

"I'm not saying I've got this thing completely whipped, but yeah, I'm learning a lot about good eating habits and exercise."

What should she say next? She brushed a strand of hair off her face and gazed down at a stream of people under umbrellas dashing back and forth along the sidewalk.

"Holly, I want to ask a favor. If it's inconvenient or if you're busy, I'll understand."

"What is it?"

"Could you come to the airport and pick me up when I get home?"

Chapter Twenty

For the last week, Holly vacillated between irritation with Jess and a desire to see his handsome face. Today, the day of his arrival, irritation was the mood of the day. She grabbed her purse from the hall table. Why couldn't Jess have asked Tim or Margaret or even his father to pick him up? Why her? For a brief moment, she'd searched for a scrap of hope for their friendship but couldn't find any. She hadn't seen or talked to him in months. He probably thought he could call her, and she'd come running back.

She fumed as she took the elevator to the parking garage, Jess's car still in his old parking place.

Traffic on Interstate 5 wouldn't pick up until later in the day, so she made good time. The exit to the SeaTac Airport veered off the freeway.

Holly entered the lane leading to short-term parking. An image of Jess lying in a hospital bed popped into her mind, rolls of flesh encompassing his waist, the double chin, his giant calves, an IV dripping in his arm. Why couldn't he see none of that mattered? She'd been in tune with his soul and his spirit.

Whatever. Now those feelings for him were lost. Right?

She parked and made her way to baggage claim where they'd agreed to meet. Visitors could watch the *down* escalator bring passengers from the gates next to the claim area.

As hard as she tried to remain calm, her heart raced. How would she react to him? What would he say to her?

For the third time, she glanced at her watch. Jess's flight arrived fifteen minutes ago. A loud shrill cut the air, and the baggage carousel began its circular route. A blinking sign indicated Jess's flight.

Her hands turned to ice cubes as she stared at the sea of humanity advancing down the escalator. A woman with a fussy baby, two men in suits, an elderly couple smiling at each other, a shoddy looking guy with a guitar case slung over his shoulder, a well-built man with pale blue eyes and a handsome face.

Her heart bounced out of her chest. Jess stepped off the escalator. A slow smile crossed his face as he waved. Where was the Jess she knew? Another man strolled across the floor. A new, slimmer Jess appeared at least eighty pounds lighter.

Her mouth fell open. A hunk coasted toward her.

~

Jess held his briefcase in one hand and shouldered his carryon. The passage led to his gate. The corridor's lengthy hall for international flights would take him to baggage claim and the main part of the airport. Five months ago he would've dreaded the walk. Though the long flight tired him, he strolled on, thankful he'd found a nonstop. The water fountain, sounding like a gurgling brook, brought a smile to his face. Welcome to Seattle.

The outcome with Vauxhall had been a positive one. He thrust his shoulders back. With the loose ends wrapped up, management expressed their satisfaction with the results. The personnel who would work with his application learned quickly, though he'd given them plenty of time.

Jess breathed a sigh. Jim had told him to take a couple of weeks off. Would the time give him the opportunity to win Holly's favor again?

It wouldn't be necessary to stop at the gift shop with the items from Washington State. He already had something for Holly. What he brought her lay safely in his coat pocket. There hadn't been a moment in his three and a half month stay in Europe when he hadn't thought of her.

He shifted his briefcase to his other hand as he skirted a mom pushing a screaming baby in its stroller. The noise didn't help his nerves. What if Holly refused to consider a relationship with him? Or maybe she had a boyfriend. He wouldn't blame her. He'd treated her badly.

Would his fit body make any difference to her? For the first time in years, he could see his feet and didn't lose his breath with every movement. The muscles he'd developed working out made him kind of proud.

The escalator took him to baggage claim. A sudden rush of joy filled his heart. At the bottom and a short distance away, Holly scanned the moving stairs, no doubt looking for him. She was more beautiful than he remembered, her hair down around her shoulders and her green eyes sparkling. The sight of her left him unhinged.

He stepped off the last stair. *Holly in his arms.* The moment had almost arrived.

A look of disbelief crossed her face.

He'd expected her reaction. She hadn't seen him since he'd slimmed down.

A woman wrestling with a baggage cart darted in front of him. Stopping a moment, he allowed the traveler to pass then closed the gap between them. He set his briefcase beside him and gazed into her eyes. When he slipped his arms around her, pulling her close, he knew how much he still cared.

"Holly." A fresh scent surrounded him. He could have held her forever.

Hands braced against his chest and pushed him away. She looked down at her shirt then smoothed a wrinkle.

"I'm happy to see you." He stepped back and stood straighter.

She spun toward the carousel. "We'd better watch for your luggage."

~

A flush of anger moved through Holly's chest. How dare Jess walk off the plane and hug her like nothing had ever happened, like he never told her to get lost after she showed him her prosthesis.

When he held her in the past, there'd been softness to his body which matched his heart. Before, Jess attracted her because he was a godly Christian man. Despite his size, he took her breath away when he kissed her. Now, fit and brash, he'd assumed she wanted his embrace. And why? Because he was in shape. She could care less about this new man. Yet she couldn't deny the warmth flooding her limbs.

The audacity of him to think they'd just pick up where they'd left off before his collapse. She tensed her shoulders while resentment built in her stomach. More than that, she couldn't risk giving herself to him now. He was a gorgeous specimen of a man who wouldn't want a woman with a partial leg. He might say it'd be okay, but she knew better. She could never grow her leg back the way he could get in shape.

Jess followed her to the carousel marked with his flight number.

The passing luggage circled yet she had no idea what his looked like. She sensed him behind her, and his warm breath fell on her neck. Then he reached around her and pull a bag off. He lifted the handlebar as he set the brown leather suitcase upright on the rollers.

"My car is close to the entrance of the parking garage." Holly barely glanced at Jess as they walked along the picture window to the glass elevator.

Jess grasped her arm to restrain her.

She curved toward him.

"Can I take you to dinner at Thirteen Coins? I'd like to talk."

Doubts assailed her, but maybe he deserved a chance to fill in the blanks. "Yes, I suppose you're hungry after your flight."

"Actually, I need a chance to get some things cleared up between us. Will you please give me the opportunity to explain? After that, if you want nothing more to do with me, I'll abide by your decision."

Behind Jess, the luggage carousel turned. She nodded. "I'd like to hear what you have to say. But like those bags spinning around and around, I think I want off this ride."

~

Jess cringed. What was wrong with Holly? Women. He couldn't always figure out what was going on in her brain.

She pulled off International into the parking lot of Thirteen Coins.

What had he been thinking? She probably hadn't forgiven him for the night he asked her to leave his apartment, and he never asked for her forgiveness before he left. He'd gone without a word -- had only thought of himself.

The host led them past dark-paneled walls toward the back. A glowing candle lamp sat in the middle of the table at each leather booth. He scooted in across from Holly.

The menu had some healthy choices -- his old way of eating gone. Even ice cream didn't tempt him anymore. Baked chicken with boiled potatoes and green salad sounded good.

After the meal arrived, Jess reached for Holly's hand to say the blessing, but she pulled away. His empty palm remained open on the table. "Lord, thank you for a safe trip. Glorify Your name in our lives and Lord, we ask you to bless this food."

The black coffee the server brought took a little of the chill off the cold treatment he received from his former friend. He had to face the situation sooner or later. "Holly?"

She twisted her fingers as she'd done during her first

service at Woodlyn Fellowship.

"Holly, please look at me."

She lifted sad eyes for a second but glanced down at her lap again.

"How have you been?"

"Okay." She continued to wring her fingers.

"How's work? The patients giving you a hard time?"

She studied something over his shoulder. "No, everything's fine."

This was a lot harder than he'd anticipated. "Holly, please. I need to talk to you."

She shrugged.

"I've had a lot of time to think." He'd have to go on even if she wouldn't look at him. "Before my collapse, my life was a mess. It took the grace of God to straighten me out."

He bared his soul to her, and she seemed so indifferent. He rubbed his forehead. "By His power, I'm free. My body is shrinking down to a normal size, for the first time in years since I gave up drinking." His throat tightened. "That night, when you showed me your leg, I loved you even more, but I couldn't strap you to my dysfunction. All this, the diet, the exercise, the change in lifestyle, I was able to do it for two reasons. I wanted to be the man God desires for His service and..." He paused, his attention trained on Holly.

With her jaw set so tightly, he didn't know if she wanted to cry or to hit him.

"I know I hurt you when I all but threw you out of my apartment. My irrational thinking prompted my words. I was selfish and gave no thought for your feelings. Please forgive me. I'm begging you, Holly.

Will you forgive me?"

For the first time since they sat down, Holly directed her gaze toward him. "I'm happy you've gotten a handle on your diet, and you're looking very trim. I'll forgive you, too, Jess, if you'll tell me one thing."

"Anything. What is it?"

"The second reason that prompted you to overcome your lifestyle."

He smiled. "I've thought so much about this. The night you said you loved me, and I told you I wished I could say the same. Well, I've finally arrived at a place I can say it." Jess reached for Holly's hand. She didn't pull back this time. "I love you, Holly. I have for a long time. I've just been unable to tell you."

She covered her face with her other hand.

"The second reason I was able to overcome my addictions is because I wanted to be the husband God desires me to be. May I be so bold as to ask you, do you still love me?" He held his breath.

Holly gazed at him with her jade green eyes, her freckles adorning her petite nose. "No, Jess. Not anymore. It's over for us."

~

Holly couldn't look at Jess when she pulled up into the parking garage. He retrieved his suitcase from her trunk and followed her to the elevators. She couldn't help but remember the day months ago when they'd been suspended in space, and he'd prayed for her.

The elevator dinged and stopped on *Five*. She stepped out through the doors without looking back.

"Thanks for the ride home," Jess called.

Did she hear a catch in his voice?

She rushed toward her door and hurried inside. Her leg hurt. She removed her prosthesis and sank down on the couch. A relationship with Jess would never work. If they were married, he'd only get tired of her once he saw her hobble around the house on her crutches or the way she struggled to get in and out of the bathtub or shower.

Life crumbled before her. The confines of the apartment became too restrictive. She hooked the crutches under her arms. With a raincoat and umbrella, she moved through the hall and out the entrance, the door closing behind.

The kissing swing in the garden would be deserted and damp, but she needed to say good-bye. She took the elevator to the lobby. A few people glanced at her with the crutches, only one foot visible under her jeans. She met their stares and continued on, surprised after all this time, her handicap was no big deal.

The sliding double doors opened. She hobbled through and turned left on the other side of the building. The familiar boxwood hedges and the poplar trees created a path to the gardens. Tulips popped up in the planters in the enclosed area.

The wind and rain had covered the swing with leaves and moisture. She brushed at them, clearing a space to sit. Her back to the swing, she hopped a step and sank down, leaving her crutches propped up on the side. The umbrella remained open over her head as she pushed herself with one foot.

Jess's healthy body brought her happiness. He'd found freedom, and she wished him the best. Before she knew it, she'd hear from Margaret. His sister would tell her how Jess found a new girlfriend, gorgeous and shapely like he deserved. Holly swiped away an unexpected tear.

"Hey, Snow White. Is this swing for a princess, or can anyone sit, even an ogre?"

The handsome man she'd abolished from her life stood before her. The vision of the well-toned muscles sent her senses reeling. "It's a free country for princess and ogre alike."

He settled next to her, no longer her big teddy bear. The bench provided plenty of room for the both of them. He gazed straight ahead at the poplar trees. Then in slow motion he revolved to her. "Holly, I don't blame you for saying you no longer have anything for me after the way I treated you, not calling you for so long." His gaze traced her face. "You said you forgave me, but I'm asking you to look deep in your heart and find a scrap of feelings you used to have. If you do, I'm willing to wait until you find more, maybe someday saying you love me again." His eyes filled with moisture. "I'll be right here for as long as it takes."

No use in denying it. Holly wiped away the tear on her cheek. Her love hadn't gone anywhere, but neither had her doubts. "You're so fit now, and more handsome than ever. I don't think any woman could resist you. We'd be fine for a while, then you'd get tired of a girlfriend or wife with a prosthesis."

"Is that what this is about? You loved me when I was sick and obese, always told me you saw the person inside. I cherish the person *I* see inside of you. Besides, God doesn't look on our outward appearance, but He sees our heart. He see you as flawless."

Holly gasped at the words.

"And what's more." His eyes sparkled as they searched hers. "There's a hot, curvy woman on the outside, too." He sucked in a deep breath. "A couple of times I had to go home and take a cold shower after my lips were on yours. Just the memory of it..." He gave a short whistle. "Is it okay if I kiss you? After all, this is our kissing bench."

She took a quivering breath. Life without this man -- she couldn't entertain the thought. A nod gave permission.

Jess trailed his finger down her neck and smoothed his lips over hers.

When he pulled away, the smile on his handsome face sent her heavenward. His finger traced little circles on her cheek. Heat traveled from her chest to her stomach when his lips brushed her forehead and journeyed to her nose. She could barely breathe as his warm mouth tickled her neck behind her ear.

How could she have ever doubted him? He brushed feather light kisses against her lips. Her heart beat wildly as Jess's hands caressed her back. As their kiss grew deeper, his embrace tightened. Her arms slid around a more slender middle.

Once again, Jess stole her heart.

Finally he sat back in the chair. "I brought you something from England, but if you can't accept it now, or maybe never, I'll understand."

She had an inkling of what he wanted to give her. "I fibbed when I said I didn't have feelings. I haven't changed my mind about you. The first day you kissed me here in this swing, I knew I loved you."

He reached in his coat pocket and pulled out a velvet box.

Holly's heart wrenched. She placed her hand on his, and pushed the box from her sight. She couldn't bear to be so close to happiness and have it taken from her by her next admission. "I -- I have something I need to tell you. It may change your mind about me."

"You can tell me anything." His sweet words did nothing to alleviate her doubt.

"Something happened in college." She prayed this revelation wouldn't ruin everything. "When Zack and I- -"

He placed a finger to her lips. "You've already told me about it. It's okay."

She choked the words out. "Yes, but I didn't tell you all of it." He had to know. "The night I lost my leg," she squeezed her eyes shut. "I lost my baby to a miscarriage. I've never been able to forgive myself for it until now."

His face didn't express the shock she'd anticipated. Instead he reached for her hand. "I'm so sorry for your loss, but Holly, the Lord has forgiven you for the old life you led in college. If I couldn't put it aside, I wouldn't be the husband God intends me to be for you. If He's forgiven you, how can I hold what happened against you? Past. It's all in our past."

Jess slid from the protection of the umbrella. Rain fell on his hair. He blinked moisture out of his eyes and opened the box, revealing an exquisite marquise-cut diamond ring set in white gold.

She gasped.

"Holly Harrison. God is my witness. I love you. I want with all my heart for you to be my wife."

Rain soaked Jess, from his head to his coat. She couldn't keep him on his knees on the wet grass with raindrops splashing his face. "Yes, Jess. My answer is yes, I want to marry you."

A gigantic smile appeared on his lips as he rose from the ground, not groaning and wheezing like he used to, and settled beside her. He held the tip of her finger, slid the ring on, and kissed her hand. Before she could speak, he covered her lips with his.

He nuzzled her hair. "I'm taking you to the Space Needle tomorrow night, and we can talk about wedding plans. We old folks don't have any reason to wait around." Then a broad smile spread over his face. "Those few weeks the church brought me meals, did you participate?"

Holly gave him a shy nod.

"Let me guess. You were my breakfast chef. Right?"

Holly raised an eyebrow. "How did you know?"

"Remember those little scriptures you'd stick in the sack with my delicious food?"

She nodded with wide eyes.

"The notepads were the same design as the paper you wrote on when you gave me your phone number. And a lot of the scriptures were the ones we heard that first time you went to church with me."

Holly laughed. "When you called me Snow White and said I was lovely, but the handsome prince wasn't handsome, I disagreed with you. The prince was and still is the most handsome and captivating man I know. I love you, Jess Colton."

JUNE FOSTER

Chapter Twenty-One

The small room off the sanctuary served its purpose with plenty of room to get ready. Holly glanced at her image in the mirror. A bride wearing a strapless white wedding dress and long hair held back by a gardenia flower clip smiled at her. She, Marcela, and Diana couldn't have made a better choice of a gown.

Maybe she should ask her sister to pinch her. The day she'd prayed about from the moment she'd fallen in love with Jess Colton had finally arrived.

Diana squeezed Holly's arm. "I can't believe you're going to be married in a few minutes."

She embraced her sister, taking care not to mess up their hairdos the sweet stylist worked on so hard. "Thank you for standing up with me as my matron of honor."

"I wouldn't want to be any place else today." Diana beamed.

Holly tried to relax and enjoy the day, but her fluttering heart had other plans. "Red is so sweet for offering to give me away. I only wish Mom would've come."

"I know, honey." Diana's gaze shimmered. "But Red was honored, more than I can say."

Marcela and Diana had never looked more beautiful. Marcela's dress matched Diana's, only a lighter shade of rose. A soft knock sounded at the door, and she opened it.

"Are you ladies ready?" The head usher gave her a shy grin.

Marcela nodded. "I think you have an anxious groom awaiting you at the altar, *hija*." She held the door open.

Marcela and Diana led the way through the doorway leading into the sanctuary of Woodlyn Fellowship. The soft tones of the Wedding March played. Her friend took a step inside, and Diana followed. Red linked his arm in hers. Not much for words, he gave her a little wink as the tones of the song intensified.

The wedding guests stood and turned to watch her. Holding onto Red, Holly floated into the sanctuary and down the aisle.

Jess stood at the altar facing her, a wide grin on his face. For awhile, she'd doubted, but in only a few moments, she would begin her life as Mrs. Jess Colton.

~

Jess couldn't contain his happiness. If she'd made him wait one more day, he might've begged her to elope. But soon, his bride would meet him at the altar. The musical tones of *The Wedding March* filled the sanctuary. Marcela and Diana made their way to the front of the church carrying bouquets of daisies and tulips. As the volume of the music rose, his bride stepped forward, arm-in-arm with Red.

"Well, Jess. Are you ready to be a married man?" Pastor Downing said before attaching a microphone to his collar.

"You, bet." Jess didn't take his eyes off Holly. He shifted to the left, his gaze still on his bride and whispered to Tim Garrett, his best man, standing next to him in a double-breasted tux identical to Jess's. "Hey, guy, you'll be doing this one of these days."

Tim gave a quiet laugh. "Yeah, sure. I can't keep up with myself much less a wife."

"Well, if you ever do, I hope you'll let me stand up for you."

"You got it." Tim clasped a hand on Jess's shoulder and released it as Holly stood in front of the pastor.

"Who gives this woman to this man?" Pastor Downing asked.

"Her mother, her sister, and I do." Red announced.

Holly passed her bouquet to Diana.

Jess's heart soared with anticipation as he moved beside Holly to take their vows. He thanked God for all He'd done in their lives. God allowed Jess to coax Holly back to Himself and a place of forgiveness. He used this beautiful woman to draw him to sanity and a healthy new life.

When, finally, he heard Pastor Downing's words, "I now pronounce you husband and wife," he praised God. They'd belong to each other for as many years as their gracious Lord would allow.

"Jess, you may kiss your bride." Pastor Downing smiled.

Jess winked at Holly. "I will. Now, and every chance I get." He pulled her to him and touched his lips to hers.

The End

Dear Reader, I pray you enjoyed Jess and Holly's story. Like Jess in Flawless, June has struggled with weight and eating in a healthy manner. If you find yourself carrying unwanted pounds, don't lose hope. Like Jess, you can find freedom from overeating. Or in Jess's case, a food addiction. As Jess did, confess the obsession as sin and seek God's help. Connect with others who struggle and turn it all over to God. The Lord's blessings.

Coming soon: Book 2 in the Woodlyn series: Out of Control.

Pastor Tim Garrett must learn to manage his angry outbursts, or he could lose it all - his job as a youth pastor and the woman he loves. Roxanne Ratner can't fall back on old habits of holding on to a guy. After she tempts Tim to sin, she seeks his forgiveness. Can God cool Tim's angry heart and teach Roxanne true beauty lies within?

About the author:

An award-winning author, June Foster is a retired teacher with a BA in education and MA in counseling. Her characters find themselves in tough situations but overcome through God's power and the Word. She writes edgy topics wrapped in a good story.

June is married with two children and ten grandchildren. She and her husband traveled all over the US for twelve years in the family RV. When not writing, June loves to go to the gym, cook healthy meals, visit with family, and attend church. Find June online at junefoster.com.

www.ingramcontent.com/pod-product-compliance
Lightning Source LLC
LaVergne TN
LVHW012016060526
838201LV00061B/4334